What the critics are saying about:

HUNTED contains two short stories that are sexually graphic and some material may be offensive to readers. But, if you are a true fan of erotic romance then HUNTED is for you.

THE HUNTED

"THE HUNTED features two deliciously interesting stories of women being hunted and captured. I thoroughly enjoyed both stories and was fascinated with each of the author's characters. Amy was a woman who took no prisoners...well maybe just one. Peggy was torn between returning home, to staying with Geirwolf. THE HUNTED is well-written and very hot. Get out the asbestos gloves while reading these erotic romances." - *Michelle Gann, The Word on Romance*

Wanted: Kept Woman
By J. W. McKenna

"Wanted: Kept Woman was a very good read! ...Suzanne can't believe how lucky she is to meet Brian. He's smart, sexy, and a little adventurous. Their attraction leaps off the pages and keeps the reader anxious to find out what happens...J.W. McKenna has crafted a wonderful read." – *Sarah, Fallen Angel Reviews*

Breeding Ground
By Jaid Black

"Jaid Black's BREEDING GROUND is wonderful. It is a science fiction story of the highest caliber and a love story with sex that leaves you hot and wanting more." – *Miaka, Romance Junkies*

Discover for yourself why readers can't get enough of the multiple award-winning publisher Ellora's Cave. Whether you prefer e-books or paperbacks, be sure to visit EC on the web at www.ellorascave.com for an erotic reading experience that will leave you breathless.

WWW.ELLORASCAVE.COM

THE HUNTED
An Ellora's Cave Publication, September 2004

Ellora's Cave Publishing, Inc.
1337 Commerce Drive, Suite 13
Stow OH 44224

ISBN #1419950177

Other available formats: MS Reader (LIT) Adobe (PDF),
Rocketbook (RB), Mobipocket (PRC) & HTML

Edited by *Tina Engler*
Cover art by *Darrell King*

THE HUNTED:

Trackers
By J.W. Mckenna

&

Besieged
By Jaid Black

TRACKERS

J.W. McKenna

Chapter 1

Amy Dellacroix scanned the room, trying to determine the energy level of her students this quarter. Well, technically, they weren't *her* students—she was the low-paid graduate assistant, teaching in place of Everett Birch, the well-respected anthropology professor at San Francisco State University. The esteemed professor wouldn't be caught dead here, she mused. Being July, he was out on another dig.

Amy saw several sleepy students in the back of the class. College students, as everyone knows, are nocturnal. Because it was just after 9 a.m., most of the students would have preferred to remain in bed.

Taking her class roll book, she casually strolled up the wide passage separating the two groups of seats to the top row. "Asher," she said, getting a quick response from her left. She ran down the roll call, walking back down the passageway toward the lectern. From that point on, they were hers.

Today's lesson centered on the Piltdown Man Hoax, an incident that had been perpetrated by English anthropologists and exposed in the early 1950s. She explained how the promised glory of a new discovery can corrupt those without unbending integrity. Amy told them this rogue incident occurred when an unknown person or persons had placed a human skull with an ape's jaw in a gravel pit near Hastings, England in an effort to make the "missing link" discovery credible.

A student in the second row raised his hand. She fought hard not to roll her eyes. "Yes, Mr. Binder?" she asked dryly.

"Isn't it true that *all* of the findings of early man were faked in order to propagate the lie that we developed from apes?" he said challengingly. "To thwart the truth–that God created man in His image?"

Amy sighed. "I teach anthropology, Mr. Binder, based on science. I make no judgments about evolution versus creationism, okay? They aren't mutually exclusive," she said emphatically. "I'd prefer that you concentrate on the course material as presented."

Fortunately for Amy, there were no further outbursts. It was as if he had said his piece and now was happy to have it on record—again—that he didn't believe a word of her lectures. With an attitude like that, she expected him to fail the exams.

Amy continued the lecture, trying to put scientific discoveries in perspective in a history that was dusty and irrelevant to them today. She knew that the only way they would learn was by rote memorization. Few would understand how all the pieces fit together. That would take at least one summer on a dig.

She wished she could have gone with the professor this year. Amy had spent five weeks in Montana's badlands last year and Birch convinced her that it was best she stayed behind to teach. "No one's better qualified that you, Amy. Besides, think of how it will look on your resume," he had said.

Amy was no fool. She knew the real reason. The professor, in his late 40s, had an eye for the youngest students. Amy was last year's model. Their brief but torrid affair burned out on the slopes of the Badlands, hip deep in T. Rex bones. Amy wasn't the wide-eyed student she used to be, so it didn't really bother her to be replaced. Besides, the sex hadn't been all that great. She needed a younger man in her life, just as the age-defying Everett Birch needed a younger woman in his.

After class, she graded papers for a little more than an hour, then headed out to meet her friend Christy for lunch at Magoo's, a trendy bistro on San Francisco's north side. In the parking garage, she absently noted that a white van was parked next to her car.

She looked closer. There was a dent in the right rear quarter panel. Could it be the same vehicle that had been parked outside of her apartment house most of the week?

Her breathing stilled. Was it just a coincidence that it was here now?

Holding her lesson plan to her chest, Amy shakily reached into her purse for the pepper spray she always carried. She walked around the far side of her car, checking the cab of the van. It was empty.

Sighing with relief, she dismissed her fears. She replaced the pepper spray with her keys and approached the driver's side of her car, mumbling to herself that she couldn't wait to get to Magoo's.

A sliding door opened behind her. She whirled, startled, a scream in her throat.

A body pressed up against hers. A damp cloth was forced over her nose and mouth, cutting off her air, instinctively making her gasp. Her heart thumping like mad, she inhaled sharply, trying to unleash her scream. But the futile effort came too late.

Amy breathed in cloying fumes as the world went dark...

Chapter 2

Amy awoke in a bed in an unfamiliar room. She tried to remember how she had gotten here, but her mind was fuzzy. One aspect of her condition was immediately clear, however — she was naked under the covers. She peered out, looking for her clothes. They were nowhere to be found.

She fought panic. *Okay, there's a good explanation for this. Maybe I'm dreaming. Maybe I'm —*

She swallowed against the lump in her throat. She was fooling herself and she knew it.

Amy looked around. Besides the bed, the room held very little furniture: a chair, a small table, a lamp. Mounted on one wall was a flat-paneled TV screen, turned off. In one corner, she spotted a camp toilet. A porcelain washbasin sat on a shelf beside it, with a china pitcher. Nothing else.

No wait — that wasn't true. Above the TV screen, she spotted a camera, recording her every move. She bit her lip, her heartbeat kicking up. *Oh, please, God, get me out of here!*

There was one door, but no windows. To reach the door, she'd have to get out of bed, exposing herself to the camera. "That'll be the day," she muttered to herself as she sat upright, pulling the sheet tight around her. She yanked it free of the bed and stood up, wrapping it around her like a toga. She strode to the door and tried the knob.

It was locked, of course.

"Damn it," she said softly, looking up at the camera. She wanted to smash it. She went to the chair and tried to pick it up instead, surprised to find it was bolted to the floor. So was the table.

"Hello, Amy," a voice said, startling her. She jerked around, trying to find the source. It must be coming from a speaker hidden somewhere on the walls or ceiling, she thought, wide-eyed. "Do not be alarmed. No real harm will come to you," the voice continued.

No real harm? What the hell did that mean?

"You've been invited to play a game with us. Regardless of the outcome, you will be returned to your hometown safely. Please allow me to explain the rules." The voice was soothing, almost hypnotic. The man was well educated, she could tell.

Her anger boiled up. She supposed she should have felt fright instead, but there it was. "Stop! I want to go home NOW! You've kidnapped me. That's a federal offense. Twenty-five years to life. If you return me now I *might* not press charges. But I want my clothes back and I want to go home, do you understand?"

The voice went on, ignoring her. "The rules are simple. You are to be the prey in a non-lethal hunt undertaken by six men who have paid me a certain amount of money to participate. I emphasize 'non-lethal.' The object is to capture you, not to harm you.

"In the morning, you are to be released, out the front door of this hunting lodge. You will find that this lodge is in the middle of a large wooded area, approximately three miles in any direction from the borders. Somewhere out along that border are two 'safety boxes' that are similar in appearance to London phone booths—you know, those large bright red enclosures? They are easy to spot. You will be given a five-minute head start. If you reach one of the boxes and manage to get inside before you are captured, you win. If you fail to reach a box before the men capture you, you lose."

Amy stood there listening, her anger quickly turning into fear. Why did they want to hunt her? What would happen to her if she was captured? "No," she said quietly to the walls. Her throat was dry, parched. "I won't be chased down like an animal."

"That, of course, is your choice. But please let me continue. If you win, you will take home fifty thousand dollars in cash. If you lose, you will still go home five thousand dollars richer — after the men extract a small penalty."

She blinked. Was this some kind of sick joke? "What do you mean, 'a small penalty'?"

"The men will have won the right to have sexual relations with you — with condoms, of course. We don't want any surprises. The first man who reaches you will be given first dibs, so to speak. The others will follow, if they wish."

She stood there, numb, as the voice continued.

"They also will be awarded your pelt. In other words, they will be allowed to shave all the hair from between your legs. In the event you lose, the hunters like to leave here with a little reminder of their adventure after you've been returned home."

My god! These men are crazy!

And that quickly, her fear again evolved into anger. "No way! I refuse to play your stupid, sick, illegal game. And I can assure you, you all will be charged with kidnapping, assault and battery, and, if necessary, rape. I hope you all end up in prison for the rest of your lives!"

"I doubt you will be able to identify us. We will all be wearing masks. We've done this a number of times and no one has ever been able to find us, let alone charge us with anything. But please, there's more. If you choose not to participate, you will forfeit all money. In that event, the men will be allowed to have sex with you *and* shave you. And, as an additional penalty, they will shave your head."

His words stunned her into silence. She could see how carefully they'd thought this out. Who wouldn't run rather than have six men rape you, then come at you with razors? The very thought made her privates tighten up. Amy reached up and touched her hair protectively. *They wouldn't, would they?*

She fought her panic with cold, calculated anger. "How many times have you done this?"

"That's confidential. I can say that it's proven to be very popular."

"You just find some poor girl, kidnap her and bring her here, just like that?"

"Yes, that is correct."

She realized she didn't have much choice if she was going to get away from here. Running was better than being trapped in this room any day of the week. Besides, she reminded herself, she just might be able to escape. Run for the fences and keep going, flag down a cop. She was a strong, athletic woman. She could do this.

Then a thought struck her. "Where are my clothes—I need my clothes for this."

"Oh, no. That's part of the game. You are to run naked. However, we will give you a pair of tennis shoes to protect your feet. We want to give you a fair chance after all. Not much fun otherwise."

Chapter 3

Amy couldn't catch her breath for a moment. Naked! Just like that movie she saw on TV one day when she was at home sick. What was it? "Naked Man" or "Naked Runner"? A man was stripped by natives and given a head start before a group of African natives came after him, intent on killing him. Somehow, he had managed to survive. *Of course, it was just a movie.*

Amy thought of herself as in pretty good shape. She had played volleyball all four years of college. She ran regularly. Her body could be called lean and muscular. Her breasts were not so big as to get in her way. So could probably outrun some rich yahoos, she figured.

"I also need to inform you of the capture devices the men will employ."

Capture devices? "I thought you said I wasn't to be harmed!"

"These are non-lethal weapons. Two of the men will have tranquilizer rifles, with a range of about fifty to sixty yards. They will be given just two darts each. The dart contains a mild, quick-acting sedative that is not intended to knock you out, but it will slow you down so that you can be captured. It should wear off within a half-hour or so. The prey often find that it makes the experience of their capture that much more bearable."

She just bet it did. Amy felt a ripple of fear go through her as she imagined being drugged, then held down, unable to defend herself as the men assaulted her.

"Two of the men will carry bolo guns," the voice continued. "These look like shotguns. They fire three rubber balls connected by strong cords. They have a range of about thirty to forty yards. The object is to fire at the legs, causing the balls to wrap around them and trip the prey. These men also will have two cartridges each."

She stood there unmoving, not knowing what to do or say.

"Finally, two men will carry net guns. They are like oversized, short-barreled shotguns. They fire a netting material that harmlessly wraps you up for capture. It's a short-range device, good for about twenty-five yards. For that reason, the men are given only one cartridge. The weapons are handed out in a blind draw, so no one can claim the advantage."

She stood there, wrapped up in her sheet, imagining it was a netting, fired from a gun, enclosing her, trapping her. She didn't want to be here, she didn't want to run naked through the woods for the twisted sexual gratification of a bunch of horny rich men. She was more scared than she had ever been in her life. But she wanted to go home and it seemed the only way out was through.

The fifty thousand dollars would help her out quite a bit right now, she knew. She hadn't been able to find a job in her field since she graduated and was resigned to waiting tables and teaching an odd class or two until something came along. With the money…

Oh Christ, who cared about the money? She just wanted out of here. She was scared, but determined. She desperately wanted to win this sick hunt. Then she'd see the men arrested, if she could.

"It is now 7:15 p.m. Dinner will be brought to your room shortly. You will be awakened at 7 a.m. for breakfast. The contest will begin promptly at eight."

"Wait," she said, hoping he hadn't already cut her off. "How do I know you'll keep your word. About the money or anything else? How do I know you aren't just saying all this to get women to cooperate?"

"Ah, a skeptic. Not surprising, considering. To ensure we play fair, we record our hunts. You may observe."

With that, the TV on the wall flickered to life. There were shots of masked men running through the brush, carrying strange weapons. She quickly identified the tranquilizer rifles. She saw one man with an almost comical weapon and surmised it was the net gun because of the oversized barrel.

His voice carried over the noises on the tape. "Each hunter has a small video camera mounted on his shoulder. The images are radioed to the lodge, where they are captured on videotape. The pictures you are seeing were culled from several hunts."

On screen, a naked blonde woman bolted from the bushes screaming and ran across the screen. A man aimed something at her and fired. She heard a strange fluttering noise and saw the girl stumble and fall, legs pinned together. That must've been the bolo gun, Amy thought. The men closed in quickly on their prey.

Another scene, another girl—a brunette. She seemed far away, running hard through a meadow, heading for the safety of the trees. A man in the foreground aimed and fired. The girl jerked but kept running. After a few minutes, she slowed and the men began to catch up to her. She tried to climb a tree, but her limbs became uncoordinated. Finally she fell, screaming, into the arms of her captors.

Another blonde woman was seen running toward a hidden man, his camera viewing through wind-swept leaves. Amy could see she had large breasts that were flapping as she pumped her arms and legs, terror written on her face. Amy watched two other men closing in behind her, both wearing strange masks. The woman was startled when the man jumped up from his hiding place and fired his gun at her. She screamed as a net closed around her, dropping her to the ground.

There was another scene of a girl being held down as the men wielded safety razors, squirting shaving cream, shaving her pelt, laughing and joking with each other. The woman struggled at first, then lay still, clearly afraid of being cut. The camera caught several close-ups that made Amy cringe and involuntarily squeeze her legs together.

The scene shifted quickly to something behind some bushes. As the camera approached, Amy could see it was one of those phone booths the man had described. It had glass walls, but appeared to be rather sturdy. Outside, a knot of men tried unsuccessfully to get in. Inside, a naked woman, sweating, scratched and panting hard, watched them.

"Once inside the booth, the woman is safe from the men. It locks automatically, only I have the key. I will be following with a bloodhound that will be tracking your scent. He will be on a leash, so you don't have to worry about being run down by dogs."

The scene showed a man wearing a bushman's jacket and a Lone Ranger mask parting the men, then turning to talk to them, telling them the game was over. The men cursed and pushed each other in frustration. Amy imagined that was the man on the intercom. She wondered if the men ever overpowered him and had their way with a girl, even if she had won.

As if reading her mind, the voice came again. "You don't have to worry about the men violating their agreement because they've pledged a considerable sum of money to participate. They may complain for a while, but I make sure they honor their word."

The video shifted again and Amy was looking at the woman from the phone booth, now dressed, accepting an envelope full of money. She was smiling. The camera panned in for a close-up to see her thumbing through several hundred-dollar bills. Later, that same woman was seen being led blindfolded from a van. Two men seated her on a park bench and left. The camera followed the men into the van and shot out the window back toward the woman. She was pulling off the blindfold as the van sped away.

Amy wondered if that entire scene had been faked. It easily could have been.

The last shot was of a map of the property. The hunting camp was roughly square, with the lodge placed just north of middle, she noticed. That meant it was a shorter distance to the north fence. The safety booths weren't marked, of course, but she wondered where they might be and how long she'd have to find them before the hunters closed in.

"The fence is slightly electrified, to prevent prey from climbing it. You wouldn't be killed, but you might be dazed, which would result in your immediate capture. You'll also notice the road to the lodge connects to the west side of the property. I can tell you that there are no booths in the area neaɪ the road. That's the only hint I will give you."

Chapter 4

Amy ate her dinner in silence, trying to figure out a way to escape before dawn. If she had a piece of metal, she might be able to jimmy the door. If she had a comb or a brush, she might be able to fashion a weapon.

She sighed. Hell, she might as well wish for a cell phone, so she could call the police. The room was devoid of anything she might use.

She looked at the plastic spoon he had given her. Hardly an effective weapon. The man who had brought the dinner was indeed the Bushman. He wore the same vest and Lone Ranger mask as in the video. He spoke only a few words to her, but she recognized the voice.

Amy was angry at herself for begging the man to release her, promising not to file charges if he would just let her go. Her words had fallen on deaf ears.

Now she sat, wrapped in her sheet, eating a TV dinner from a plastic plate, trying desperately to figure out how to survive this experience. The idea of men chasing her down terrified her.

A distant memory surfaced: A girls' camp, many years ago. She was 13 or 14, in the first blush of developing womanhood, experiencing a lot of strange new feelings. The girls decided to play a game, truth or dare. She had accepted their challenge. Because the girls had been asking some embarrassing questions, she chose "dare."

Susan — that was her name. Susan had organized the game. The counselors had gone to bed, leaving the girls alone in their tents. Susan came up with the dare for Amy — she would have to run naked from their tent to the latrine and back. To prove she had been there, she was to bring a handful of toilet paper back with her.

Amy hadn't wanted to do it. She refused at first and was hooted down by the other girls. "You picked! You chose dare!" They squealed. She said she wouldn't let them see her naked, no matter what the game was. So they agreed to stay in the tent and not look. To ensure she ran naked, she had to agree to let one girl go outside with her to collect her clothes. She would hold her hand over her eyes and Amy would drape her clothes over her arm.

"Just bring back the toilet paper and we'll believe you," Susan had said.

The challenge, which was designed to be humiliating, had excited Amy far more than she had let on. But then that had been a child's game, whereas this new game was so much more than that.

The latrine had been about a hundred yards from their tent — an easy jog, she'd figured. Being naked had been beyond naughty. It had made her tingle inside in a way she'd never felt before. But again, these circumstances were different than those.

Amy had gone outside with Diane, a friend she could trust. They walked down the path a short distance, then stood behind a tree. Diane, true to her word, put one arm out and closed her eyes, clasping the other hand over them to ensure she wouldn't peak. Amy had quickly stripped off her shorts and tee-shirt.

"The bra and panties, too," Diane had said, feeling the garments Amy had given her. Reluctantly, Amy had complied. She had already been barefoot.

"Okay — go!" Diane said, dropping her hand from her eyes and looking boldly at the naked girl.

Amy gasped and took off running, trying to get away from the girl's gaze. *Cheater! You peeked!* She ran like the wind toward the latrine, which sat away from the tents so the smell wouldn't bother anyone. Amy felt free and open as she ran. It was like nothing she had ever experienced before. She was practically giddy.

She approached the latrine and was about to go inside when she heard a toilet flush! *Oh my god!* She had forgotten that it easily could have been in use! Somehow, she had assumed, because it was so late, that no one would be there.

Quickly, she ducked down around the side of the structure, breathing hard. Her nipples hardened in the night air. She had odd feelings in her groin — like she had an itch between her legs. As she squatted there, waiting for the person to leave, she reached down and touched herself.

God! She was so wet! How did this happen? Why? She jerked her hand away as she heard the door open. She peered around the corner and watched as one of the counselors walked away toward their tent, her back to Amy. That was close!

Amy waited a few minutes, her ears straining to pick up any other noises from the latrine. There was silence.

With a sudden boldness, she ran around the corner and threw open the door. Thankfully, the structure was empty. She grabbed a handful of toilet paper from the nearest stall and bolted out the door and down the path.

She felt liberated! She had done it! Amy jogged back like a victorious knight returning from battle. When she approached the tent, she was not surprised — nor disappointed — to see all the girls outside, waiting for her.

She waved the toilet paper in her hand as they hooted and jeered. Amy didn't care. She'd never felt so alive as on that night. It was as if she had passed through a barrier into adulthood. She quickly snatched her clothes from Diane and ran inside to put them on.

The girls considered her a hero after that night. Not only did she successfully complete her dare, but she seemed unconcerned about her nakedness. Many of the other girls still hadn't made that transition and they admired Amy's bravery.

Now, sitting in the stark room, Amy considered the parallels. This was just like that night in camp, all over again. If that counselor had caught her, it would have been very embarrassing. But she had escaped and it made her stronger, bolder. She was determined to escape again.

Later, when she went to bed, she felt that same itch she had experienced as a young teen. Amy reached down and touched herself. Her clit was aroused, her labia wet. Hiding under the covers, safe from prying eyes, Amy brought herself to a quick orgasm.

But she knew that the stakes were different this time. Very different indeed.

Chapter 5

The next morning, Amy was up before she was called, stretching out her leg muscles. She felt exposed and imagined the man was getting an eyeful through the camera, but she no longer cared. She was angry — and she was in this to win. She'd show those bastards.

At 7 a.m., the door opened and the man she thought of as Bushman walked in. He was wearing the same bush jacket and mask.

At his side, in a leather holster, he was carrying a pistol. That sobered her. *Would they just kill her at the end, rather than risk having her as a witness?* The erotic thrill of the hunt diminished in the sober light of day.

She couldn't help but cover herself with her arms. The man paid no attention. He carried in a tray. She could smell coffee, scrambled eggs and bacon. He set the tray on the table and she jumped on it, devouring the food, slurping the coffee, her shyness forgotten.

"What shoe size do you wear?" he asked.

"Seven," she said from around mouthfuls.

He left, and returned a few minutes later with a shoebox. Inside were some rather expensive running shoes and a pair of low-cut white socks. "These are yours to keep, regardless of the outcome," he said. "I will come for you at eight."

He left without another word. He didn't seem to get any thrill from her nakedness. He must be used to it by now, she thought. Or maybe he's gay. She allowed herself a bit of nervous laughter at that thought. Her bravado was a mask, however. Inside, she quaked with fear.

* * * * *

The six men milled around nervously, even a little embarrassed, as if they had been caught peeking into their neighbors' windows. A few hung out around the coffeemaker set up at one end of the rustic lobby, waiting for the clock to strike eight.

Roger Bollinger entered, dressed for the hunt. His bushman vest and hat might've caused snickers in another setting, but here he seemed aptly dressed. Besides, the gun on his hip dissuaded any jokes. "Just a few more minutes, gentlemen," he said, then strode to the coffeemaker.

Andy Reed stepped aside to let the man pour a cup. Of all the men in the room, Andy felt the most out of place. He was pudgy, with dark curly hair that always looked like it needed a wash. He was only here because his friend and business partner, Jake Neely, had practically dragged him along. Jake said he needed to live a little, spend some of his money. God knows, they had plenty.

Jake and Andy had been friends since high school, which surprised everyone because they were so different. While Andy was the classic nerd, Jake was tall and handsome, with blue eyes that made high school girls a little weak in the knees.

Growing up in Silicon Valley, Jake lived two doors down from Andy, so they managed to find common ground for their friendship early.

Jake was impressed by Andy's grasp of computers and enjoyed going over to play the latest games. Andy's parents had been hopelessly lost when it came to what their son did, which allowed the boys a great deal of latitude.

Jake was as outgoing as Andy was shy. How he managed to stay friends with the withdrawn Andy, no one could figure. But Jake saw something in Andy that few bothered to look for: Andy was going to invent something BIG someday. Jake was sure of it. By age fifteen, the boy had seemed to know how everything worked. What would he be like when he was in college?

"With my salesmanship and your brains, we can go far," he used to tell him. They jokingly called themselves "The Two Steves" after Jobs and Wozniak, the founders of Apple Computer and kings of Silicon Valley. Jake admired Jobs' ability to reinvent his company's products to take advantage of new trends.

Sure enough, Jake had been right. He had followed Andy to Berkeley, where he could keep an eye on his friend. Berkeley was a great place for both boys. Andy had the top-notch computer lab, led by the best instructors, while Jake had the girls and frat parties. Andy got "A's" and Jake got laid. He was unconcerned about his middling grades. Jake encouraged Andy in his work and looked for commercial possibilities.

The breakthrough came when both boys were juniors. Andy developed software that doubled the speed of dial-up connections just as the FCC relaxed its rules on signal restrictions that had kept speeds below 53K.

Jake wisely secured a patent on the invention and formed a small company. Both young men dropped out of school to grow the company. Within six months, the young men were being courted by giants of the industry, all eager to buy out DialSonic Software.

At first, Jake wanted to keep their company and convinced his reluctant friend to reject the early offers. For Andy, the thrill was in the invention. He was ready to move on to the Next Big Thing. Jake came around quickly—he knew better than to try to hold Andy back.

They sold DialSonic to Qwest for $45 million—a bargain, no doubt. After paying off their seven employees, Jake and Andy split $36 million. In the eight years since, Jake had nearly doubled his share with additional investments in Andy's work, plus a few lucrative real estate deals.

Andy was richer, as he had invested in another company that Jake had taken a pass on and reaped $25 million on a $4 million investment when the company had gone public.

Now the young men could indulge themselves with the biggest houses, fastest cars, and the best-looking women around. Andy, still awkward, preferred the company of his computers. Jake was much more the ladies' man, always searching for the "perfect" woman. It was his idea that they go "on safari" after a naked woman. The idea titillated him no end. Andy was just here to please his friend.

Across the room, Levon Jackson looked around at his fellow competitors. He was the only African-American man in the room and he liked that. Jackson—no one called him Levon— enjoyed sticking his black head into good ol' boys clubs like this one. Of course, to call these men competitors was a stretch. In this game, if one won, they all won, for the reward was nearly the same.

For Jackson, however, winning was everything. Six years in the NFL will do that to a man. He had been a star cornerback for the San Diego Chargers until a knee injury ended his career. After recovering, he switched to business, earning millions for his astute investments.

Next he targeted hunting. The wall of his den at home was filled with the heads of prize-winning rams, bucks, and bear. Today, he wanted to bring the girl down and he wanted first crack at her, simply because that was the game. No sloppy seconds for him. Let the others wait in line.

At 44, Jackson felt his life was slipping away, though he worked out regularly. Every year, it got a little harder to hike up to the good hunting sites, or chase down a wounded buck. He was still ruggedly handsome, with smooth dark features under a thinning cap of hair. But for a fiercely competitive person, it was tough to lose a step.

To him, this hunt was a dream come true. It had all the elements—the thrill of hunting a very clever prey, plus the instant gratification in the win. Not only did it have the echoes of the game he used to play, it was combined with the sexual release that comes with the mounting of a good-looking woman. It was as if, after a touchdown, his team had been allowed to pull a woman out of the crowd and fuck her. What a TV ratings boost that would have been.

Nearby, two older men sat drinking coffee. One was fidgeting, spilling sugar as he broke open a packet. "So, you nervous?" Phil Simmons finally asked his older brother Steve. Steve looked up calmly from his Styrofoam cup. He could see that Phil was still rattled. He was so predictable.

"Look, Phil. For the last time, we won't get caught. Bollinger's done this a dozen times. They're drugged when captured so they don't know where they are, and we wear masks so she can't recognize us. No one will ever know. Heck, we even wear rubbers—no DNA!"

"I know, I know. It just seems so wrong, you know."

Of course it's wrong—that's the point! Steve sighed. "The girls aren't really hurt. We get a little show and they take home some money. What's the harm?"

Phil hung his head. Steve wondered how two such different people could be brothers. *We look similar, but our personalities are poles apart,* he thought. Steve was the adventurer, always looking for new challenges. Phil was the cautious one, afraid to stick his neck out.

Steve took a gamble on an untried business and made a fortune, while Phil went to work for a corporation and made a salary. Now almost half of their lives were gone.

Steve enjoyed a rich, full life, drinking the best wines, traveling the world. Phil worked for a faceless corporation all day and went home alone to his small apartment every night. Since his divorce last year, Phil felt that his life was over at age forty-seven. His older brother was determined to pull him out of his doldrums.

When Steve heard of this special hunt, he had to participate. He thought it would be the perfect gift for his brother, something to wake him up and make him appreciate life more. *God, he was such a worker bee!*

Now, as he looked across the table at him, he realized that Phil would probably wet his pants before the day was over. Or be too shy to "partake" in the reward.

"It's going to be okay, Phil. Trust me on this."

The last man in the little group sat apart from the others. Dirk Bowman was the only one who wished they could use real weapons. He would even prefer that the prey be a man—that would be more of a challenge.

As it was, this was going to be too easy. Chase a defenseless girl down and fuck her. Big deal. He'd rather give the victim a knife and make it a little sporting.

Dirk was ready for the next level of hunting. Like Jackson, he had all the right trophies. Frankly, it had begun to bore him. Chasing down a human, now that had exciting possibilities!

When Bollinger had first approached him, he had in mind a serious hunt. He felt this would be the perfect swan song to his youth. Dirk would be forty in one month. He had been so enamored by the idea, that he signed on before he fully realized what a cakewalk this was going to be.

Dirk figured they'd be done by 9 o'clock—maybe even sooner. They'd each paid fifteen thousand for this hunt. If they won, they'd get back seventy-five hundred, plus have a quick fuck. If they lost—well, that was impossible, wasn't it? That's why Dirk wished it could be made a little more challenging.

Hell, if I ran this hunt, things would be different, he thought. *And maybe I should. Bollinger doesn't have a patent on hunting humans for sport.*

"Ready for this?"

Dirk was startled to see Bollinger standing over him. "Uh, yeah, Roger, I am. Although I think it could be a little more sporting."

"Yeah? How so?"

"Well, how about we give her something to fight back with — say a net gun? Make it a little more evenly matched."

"Uh, no, Mr. Bowman. I've carefully studied this and found that this way is the best. You get the prey fighting back like that and people can get hurt."

Dirk decided not to press it. "Yeah, okay. Just wondering."

"Hey, I'm sure you'll have fun. It's a very stimulating game."

Dirk just nodded. Bollinger looked at his watch. "Gentlemen," he told the room. "Let's attach your video equipment."

The men stood still in turn as Bollinger snaked the small video camera about the size of an eraser from a fanny pack to their shoulders where they were pinned into place. The whole operation took just a few minutes. Afterwards, he showed them how their actions could be seen from the monitors in the office.

"Remember, gentlemen, you'll be monitored, so follow the rules." He glanced at his watch again. "Now it's time to draw for your weapons."

He strode over to a steel door set into a wall. Brandishing a key, he opened it. Inside the narrow closet a row of weapons gleamed. "Here they are: Tranquilizer guns, bolo guns and net guns."

Dirk recognized some paint guns along the bottom row. He knew the ranch was also used for corporate outings. Anything for a buck, he mused.

From inside, Bollinger pulled out a large coffee can. "Now you all know the rules — no one can select his weapon. All are given out in a blind draw."

Bollinger handed out slips of paper to each man and told them to write down their names. He collected each one and dropped them all into the can. Making a show of it, he rolled up the sleeve of his shirt. "The first two names will be for the net guns, with one cartridge each."

He reached in and pulled out a name. "Jake."

Inwardly, Jake groaned. He considered the net gun the most useless weapon. Nevertheless, he put on a brave face and collected it from the man.

Bollinger drew again. "Phil."

Phil actually looked pleased. Having a net gun would probably mean he wouldn't be needed during the hunt. He could just hang back with the crowd. Phil took the weapon gratefully.

"Now the bolo guns, with two cartridges each." He drew. "Jackson."

Jackson shrugged. He had wanted a tranquilizer gun, but this would do.

"Andy."

Andy wasn't even sure how to operate the gun, but he wouldn't admit that in front of Steve. As he walked back to his seat, he opened the breech and studied it, taking it apart in his head. Within a couple of minutes, he not only had figured it out, he saw ways to improve the design. *If I could take one back to my lab,* he thought, his mind elsewhere.

"Finally, the tranquilizer guns, with two darts each, go to Dirk and Steve." He handed them out. "Now, gentlemen, it's time to put on your masks. I will go get the prey."

Chapter 6

Promptly at eight, Bushman returned to Amy's room. She had used the toilet and had freshened up as best she could. Her new shoes were on her feet, laced tight. Her stomach churned. She would rather be any place — the dentist, the gynecologist — than here.

"This way," he said, gesturing to her and standing aside. Amy tried to put on a false sense of bravado. She deigned not to cover herself this time. She went through the portal ahead of him, swaggering just a little for his benefit. At least she knew her ass looked good. Inwardly, her heart thumped in her chest and her breathing felt restricted.

In the lobby of the lodge, she met her hunters for the first time. Some whistled appreciatively as she walked in, nude except for her shoes. The false swagger went out of her. These men were out to hunt her down and rape her. Amy was mortified.

The men were an odd mix — made even odder by the different masks they wore. All of the masks were spare, covering just the eyes and, in some cases, forehead, leaving the nostrils, mouth and chin open. The better to breathe, she thought.

She'd have them gasping soon enough.

From their eyes and the lines around their mouths, she guessed two were as young as thirty, another two were a little older, perhaps in their forties, while two more appeared to be well on their way to fifty. Some were outfitted for the full safari, with bush jackets and silly bush hats, while the younger ones appeared to be dressed for a pickup game of basketball, wearing shorts, tee-shirts and baseball caps.

Each of them was carrying a weapon, she noticed. She tried to memorize the masks of the men with the tranquilizer guns, as they'd be her most serious opponents. A man in a feathered mask and streaks of gray in his hair had one, as did a 40-something man with powerful arms. His puffy mask made him look like a gargoyle. She didn't like the man's eyes, she decided. They had a hard, flat look. She returned their gazes, trying not to show her fear. Unconsciously, she found herself trying to cover her nudity.

"Gentlemen, you know the rules," Bushman said. "The prey gets a five-minute head start. I will fire two shots from my pistol to let her know when we've started. My dog handler will trail her with the bloodhound on a leash to give you her direction.

"You may go ahead of us, of course. If you capture her, you may partake in your first reward—just be sure to use the condoms you've been provided. We wouldn't want any DNA mishaps, would we? When I catch up, I'll bring the shaving materials."

Amy took a deep breath.

"If she makes it to a booth, don't try to break in. Observe the rules and play fair. Remember, gentlemen, all of your actions are being recorded."

Bushman turned to Amy. "Prey, are you ready?"

It irked her that he didn't use her name. She tried to use her anger to steel herself for the ordeal ahead. "I'm ready—and my name is Amy. You should remember it when you're all arrested."

Bushman led her out to the porch. In her head, she could see the map and knew she was looking north, the shortest distance to the fence by about a quarter mile. Another man waited there, with a sorrowful looking bloodhound on a leash. This man was armed with a pistol as well, she noticed.

Suddenly, something else diverted her attention. Parked out front were three dark blue golf carts. A fourth golf cart, painted white, was parked beyond them. Their reason for being there was quite clear to her.

"Hey," she said. "You didn't say anything about the men being allowed to ride!"

Bushman smiled. "Oh? Didn't I mention that? Well, I wouldn't want any of my guests having a heart attack, now would I? But don't worry—they only have enough gas for three miles. It's carefully measured. If you stay ahead of them, they'll eventually have to go on foot as well. Besides, I think you should be able to outrun the carts. Their top speed is only about ten miles per hour.

"I'll be riding in the white cart, acting as observer." Without waiting for her arguments, he held up a stopwatch. "Go," was all he said.

Chapter 7

She stared at him for a full three seconds, not wanting to believe that the hunt had already begun. Her muscles galvanized her into action. Amy leapt off the porch and immediately cut right. She knew that most of the women would run for the closest fence, which meant she shouldn't. It was too obvious.

She had a crude strategy planned out in her head: she would run southeast, trying to meet the perimeter at an angle, then run along it to the southern border, searching for a safety booth along the way. She planned to use every minute of the five minutes she had been given. Amy decided not to zig-zag or otherwise try to fool the men or the dog. The shortest distance to the nearest booth was a straight line. She only hoped that one would appear in her path soon.

She set out on a determined lope, trying to place as much distance as possible from her hunters while not wearing herself out. The wind felt strange on her naked body, especially between her legs. It was very much like that night at camp, so many years ago.

Amy tried to gauge her direction from the sun through the trees, keeping the mental picture of her position on the map. She had covered less than a mile when she heard a shot behind her, then another. Amy figured she was still about two miles from the fence, maybe more. She kept running.

Sweat poured off her body from the heat and the exertion. She was slowing now, despite her fears and determination. She angled her direction a bit more east, so she could find the fence. She wondered now if she could outrun the men.

Amy knew that they would stay in those carts as long as possible, until she was nearly exhausted. Then it would be easy to surround and capture her. *It's a rigged game!* She wondered how many women actually won—or if there really were these so-called safety booths?

She heard the distant growl of golf carts behind her when she first spotted the fence, well off to her left among the trees. It was tall, about ten feet high, and the chain links held green, opaque strips to prevent prying eyes. Every fifty feet, a sign warned of danger. Even if it weren't electrified, it would be difficult to climb with men hot on her trail.

She jogged south, keeping her eyes out for a booth ahead of her and her ears on the men behind her. Amy heard the whir of an approaching cart almost too late and dodged, just as a dart flitted through the bushes to her right. Luck was with her—those guns were nearly silent.

One dart down, three to go, she thought.

Behind her, Steve cursed as his perfect shot went wide. "Faster," he shouted at Phil.

"I'm flooring it as it is!"

Amy was convinced that these carts could go faster than ten mph. *The asshole's a liar, besides being a cheat.* Women stood almost no chance out here. She would liked to have seen those guys run through the trees instead of ride—she would run them into the ground.

Now she would have to change her strategy in order to win.

She turned and saw two carts bearing down on her, one in front of the other. Although the first cart was faster than she was, the cart had trouble negotiating the ground through the trees. The driver constantly had to jerk the wheel to dodge debris, throwing off the aim of his passenger pointing a tranquilizer gun at her.

"Take it easy! I can't aim!" Dirk shouted to Jackson over the noise of the cart engines. He was grinning despite himself. *This was fun!*

Ahead, Amy spotted a small section of a log on the ground ahead and got an idea. Bending over as she approached, she scooped up the log, stopped and flung it in front of the cart. Jackson jerked sideways just as Dirk fired and another dart shot just wide of the mark.

Two darts down. Amy turned and ran again.

"Dammit! I gotta get outta this cart before I risk my last dart," Dirk said.

"You'll get your chance soon," Jackson replied. "We're almost out of gas."

Well off to her right, the third cart containing the younger men pulled ahead, using an open area between the trees to gain speed. She knew they were working to outflank her. She guessed correctly that they had the bolo gun and the net gun, because she knew two of the men behind her had tranquilizers.

For a brief moment, she imagined her and some of her girlfriends chasing down naked men through the woods, armed with similar weapons. "It'd serve them right," she muttered through her teeth.

The carts behind her began to close, forcing her to zigzag. That allowed the third cart to move up on her right. Her breath burst from her lungs now. She didn't know how much longer she could run like this. Amy figured the men probably had been driving for more than two miles now. If she could hang on for another mile—

She heard a strange noise that outwardly she didn't recognize, but found herself cutting hard right. It was only after she heard the whistling of the bolo balls through the air where she had been running a second earlier that she remembered the noise from the video.

Thank god for quick reactions, she thought.

The cart on her right moved just ahead of her now and veered left, closing the gap. Jake, steering with one hand as the cart slowed, aimed that strange large-bore gun at her with the other. Instinct took over and she scooped down to grab a long branch.

She ran right at him, with the stick held out. When the man fired, the net caught the point of the branch and wrapped around it. It was jerked from her hand, but she was still free.

She was so close now, Jake jerked to a stop so Andy could pull up his weapon. She jumped sideways in the air and aimed her right foot squarely at the driver's face, hoping to knock him into the second man. He yelled and held up his hands, partially deflecting her blow.

Amy hit him and fell painfully on the ground, then bounced up. It had worked: the passenger's unused bolo gun had fallen out of the cart. She grabbed it and spun away.

A dart meant for her struck Jake in the upper arm. He shouted and jerked about, yanking the dart from his arm.

Amy felt like Joan Wayne. Only one dart left. She looked over and saw a Caucasian man riding with an African-American man throw away his tranquilizer gun away in disgust.

"I can't believe I missed her!"

"Well, then, you drive. I've still got a shell left," Jackson braked the cart so they could switch positions.

Amy turned and saw one of the older men climb out of the second cart and raise his tranquilizer gun in her direction. *The last dart!* From her hip, she fired the bolo from about forty yards away and watched as the line tightened around his legs. He fell down, dropping the gun in the dirt.

Amy spun back around as the pudgy passenger behind her climbed over the groggy driver and tried to grab her. She drove the stock of the weapon into his face, splitting open his nose. Blood gushed forth from under his mask as he stumbled away, holding his nose with both hands, crying.

Amy grinned ferally. *I'll bet that guy thought this was just a game!*

The last cart was closing fast—Amy knew she would be overrun in seconds. Suddenly, it jerked to a halt. The passenger jumped out and picked up the fallen man's long gun.

"What the hell are you doing?" Steve shouted, still struggling with the cord around his legs.

"You're not using this," Dirk replied and jumped back into the cart.

The delay gave her the reprieve she needed. Amy yanked the stuporous driver out of his seat, jumped in and hit the gas. The cart roared forward. Now she was on a more even keel with these bastards.

Amy realized she was still holding the empty bolo gun and the injured man's last shell was probably in his pocket. She held onto it for a few more seconds before chucking it out the side, hoping it would get lost in the bushes.

"Dammit! She's gotten a cart!"

Dirk smiled. "Maybe this will be a real contest after all," he murmured.

One cart was about forty yards behind her, the second cart, farther behind. She knew one man still had a dart in his tranquilizer gun. Amy figured the man she'd hit with the bolo gun was probably out of the game, unless he could get untangled quickly, along with the two hunters from the cart she'd stolen.

She didn't have time to congratulate herself on her accomplishments. Amy began to zigzag slightly, just enough to throw off his aim. She kept looking for a damn booth, but she saw nothing but trees and bushes and dust.

She risked a look behind her and saw the cart of her closest pursuer sputter and die, even as hers continued to run. That surprised her until she remembered that it had been idling for a short time, using less gas.

The men jumped out, guns in hand and followed her. One of them held a long gun. She recognized a bolo gun in the African-American man's hands. Just as she approached the southern border, the gas engine on her cart sputtered, caught, sputtered again, then died.

Shit.

She didn't even wait for it to stop moving before she jumped out and ran. She had gained a little distance, but not nearly enough.

The last cart was farther behind, but still running. It had to be nearly out of gas by now too.

The brief rest in the cart had energized her, although she knew she had to be much more tired than her pursuers. Sweat poured off her body in sheets. She ran along the southern wall and was stricken to see the two men gaining on her already. The speed of the African-American man astonished her. He was leaving his partner behind.

Jackson enjoyed the pounding of his feet as he closed on the girl. He carried the bolo gun like a football. He didn't think he needed it now—he'd just come up behind her and tackle her, remind himself of old times.

Amy ran on, desperately looking for the stupid booth—if one even existed. Amy looked back and was dismayed to see that her pursuer had closed the distance between them considerably. Yet he made no effort to shoot her.

She zigzagged again, vainly searching for a booth. Just when she was sure she had been played for a fool, she spotted one ahead, a red flash between the trees. Just one hundred yards or so, she thought.

I could win this.

Dirk came out of the trees and saw the girl just ahead of Jackson. Jackson was just about to catch her. At that moment, he knew he didn't want to be second. He thought of himself as a winner—at any cost. Instinctively, he stopped, brought the gun up and fired.

Jackson never heard the whizzing of the dart that struck him in the back, just below his shoulder blade. He cried out, startled, and turned to see Dirk standing about fifty yards away.

"Sorry, man—I was aiming at her!" he shouted unconvincingly.

The bastard! I'll kill him! Jackson didn't want to let the girl go now. He turned and ran after her, fighting the heaviness in his arms and legs. *I'll deal with you later,* he mentally promised Dirk.

The booth was just forty yards away now, but Amy's legs felt like lead and her lungs were bursting. She didn't understand why the African American man hadn't caught her yet. She looked back and was startled to see the leering mouth of the hard-eyed man as he jogged past the faltering black man.

At that moment, she tripped over a log and went down hard on her side. She lay motionless, gasping, unable to move. Every muscle in her body hurt. Her remaining strength ebbed. She heard the man's heavy breathing as he approached her.

"Got you, dammit, I got you! First dibs!"

God, he sounds like a junior high school kid! Amy opened her eyes and spotted a rock near her outstretched arm. Quietly, she lay her hand next to it and waited. *Come on, you bastard, come on!* The man approached her. "Hey, little missy, you really gave us a fight." He leaned over her, breathing hard, his hand brushing her breast. "I'm really going to enjoy fucking you!"

With all of her remaining strength, Amy swung the rock at him, catching him a glancing blow on the side of his head. He fell with a guttural cry and lay on his back, moaning and cursing.

She struggled to her feet, running on pure adrenaline. She looked back to see the African American man staggering his way toward her, closing fast, his mouth set in a determined grimace. Right behind him came the two older men, puffing hard.

She turned back and saw the booth less than twenty-five yards away. She didn't have any energy left for outsmarting the men behind her or dodging their weapons. She only had a single-minded goal to reach the booth. She clawed her way toward it, half upright and half on all fours.

She had just reached the door when she heard the whizzing of the bolo and wasn't surprised when it wrapped around her legs, dropping her to the ground. Still, she didn't give up.

She crawled the last few yards, using her legs to push her torso forward. With a final burst of energy, she pulled herself over the open doorway, thrust herself inside and slammed the door with her bound-up legs. The lock clicked into place.

Immediately, there came a pounding from the outside. She was safe.

Exhausted, she let herself drift into unconsciousness.

Chapter 8

"Wake up, Amy, wake up." She thought she was home again, in her own bed. She expected her father to greet her, but the voice was wrong. She came to slowly and opened her eyes. Bushman's mask loomed over her. She recoiled and tried to get away.

"Relax, Amy, relax. You won. You're going to be fine now."

She looked around. She was back in her cell, on the bed. Small bandages covered the cuts and scrapes from her ordeal. A robe was draped over her. She pulled it around her. "I won?" she managed.

"Yes. You reached the booth safely. Of course, we have several men outside who are crying foul. You hurt one of them rather badly. And some are saying you shouldn't have been allowed to use a gun or drive a cart. For some reason, they didn't think that was part of the bargain. But as far as I'm concerned, you beat them, fair and square."

He took an envelope from his jacket. "Here. Your winnings. You've earned it." She opened it, not trusting him. Inside were dozens and dozens of one hundred-dollar bills. No, she realized, there must be five hundred of them. It was a fortune to her.

Her tongue was thick, but she had to ask: "How often do women win?"

Bushman laughed. "Actually, you're the first."

"But, the video—"

"Yes, that part was staged, I'm afraid. Otherwise, the girls would feel they had no chance at all and might quit. That wouldn't be sporting. But you've changed all that. You've proven to be a formidable opponent."

She sank back down and closed her eyes. She was exhausted. "I still think you should all be arrested. When can I go home?"

"Uh, anytime..." He paused.

She opened one eye. "What?"

"Well, the men—or I should say four of them; two of them just want to go home—wondered if you'd be willing to have a rematch. For one hundred thousand dollars."

She laughed derisively. "Not a chance in hell..."

Amy caught herself. *A hundred grand*? She bit her lip. She imagined what she might do with another hundred thousand dollars on top of the fifty she had already won. She was probably an idiot for even considering it, and no doubt the thrill of victory was still rushing through her veins, but she heard herself say, "Unless..."

He leaned forward, eager. "Unless?"

"Unless *they* agree to run naked too. And no carts."

He smiled.

Chapter 9

Bollinger gave Amy a day to rest up. It also gave Andy with his broken nose, and bookish Phil, a chance to make their escapes. Steve and Jake watched them go, each saddened that their efforts to spice up their lives had failed so miserably. Each also admitted to himself that the men would not be missed.

Wet blanket, Jake thought of his long-time friend as he waved goodbye.

Pantywaist, thought Steve of his brother.

"Come on, gentlemen, we're going to have a tremendous dinner tonight. I've flown in a top chef to cook—spared no expense!"

Jackson knew that he could afford it—they were paying for it. Because only four were playing, Bollinger had upped the cost to thirty thousand per man. After expenses, including the payouts if they won the game this time around, he calculated Bollinger would take home thirty thousand as well, if the men received their agreed-upon payout of twenty grand each and the girl got her ten-thousand-dollar consolation prize.

If the girl won and took the hundred-thousand-dollar prize, Bollinger's total would drop to twenty thousand, minus expenses. Jackson wondered if the ringleader might tip the scales their way in order to pick up an extra ten Gs. Not that it mattered.

Jackson, of course, had another agenda. He was gunning for Dirk Bowman. Cheap shots, whether in the NFL or in life, were not to be ignored.

Amy was not invited to join them for dinner at first, but Jake and Steve insisted. "Come on, she's agreed to this, it's not like it was before—where she was being held against her will. She signed the contract, didn't she?"

Yes, she had—a 17-page document that outlined the hunt, the methods of possible capture and the penalties therein. Because there were only four men, she agreed to one change—there would only be one safety booth this time. In exchange, she got them to agree to pass out only one tranquilizer gun. A net gun would also be eliminated from the selection of weapons.

She had to absolve the men of past "activities," which Amy knew was a euphemism for felonies. It was not an easy decision for her. Forgiving a kidnapping and assault takes some serious thought.

Still, she had fifty thousand in hand and a chance for a hundred thousand more. Amy felt her chances were excellent. She'd show these bastards who could run. She'd run circles around these overfed fat cats with their silly little weenies. *I hope their dicks get sunburned!*

As a final precaution, Amy was not to know their names. Each man had chosen a color that he would be identified by, an idea stolen from a Hollywood movie. Jackson had naturally chosen "Mr. Black." Steve was "Mr. Blue." Jake was "Mr. Green" and Dirk was "Mr. Red." Bollinger, the referee, chose "Mr. White."

By signing the contract, Amy released the men from having to wear the unpopular masks. They were too sweaty in the heat and limited the vision. Because it didn't matter that she saw them, the other men saw no reason why she couldn't join them for dinner.

Amy, however, refused until they gave her clothes. "No way I'm parading in front of them naked while they're fully dressed," she spat when Bollinger came into her room. "If they're dressed, I'm dressed; if I'm naked, they're naked."

The men, already a little embarrassed by the thought of them running naked tomorrow, agreed instantly that she should wear clothes to dinner. The alternative was unthinkable. She was given back the blue dress she was kidnapped in, plus her bra and panties.

Chapter 10

Striding into the dining room, shoulders back, just as she had the morning of the first hunt, Amy met the gazes of the men defiantly. She wanted to spread doubt in their minds. She studied the faces of her pursuers.

Amy was introduced to the men. There was a surreal quality to the civility present at dinner. Here she was, being welcomed like an invited guest, when tomorrow they would be hunting her down like a pack of wild dogs, with the goal of raping her.

Why did I ever agree to this? Am I a fucking idiot? Don't answer that…

Associating the faces with their colorful names wasn't difficult. Amy next tried to gauge the men to determine their level of threat to her.

Mr. Black had been the one who she thought was going to reach her first, she remembered. She still didn't know why he faltered at the end. Ran out of gas, probably. He looked as athletic as she did, only fifteen years older. She hoped he had lost some of his wind or she would be in trouble. Amy wondered what he did for a living.

Mr. Red possessed a cunning, feral look. She remembered his eyes just before she conked him on the head at the end of the hunt. Amy felt like prey when he fixed his steely eyes upon her. There was a savageness to him that none of the others possessed. She guessed that he would want revenge.

Amy realized that if either Mr. Red of Mr. Black got the tranquilizer gun, the game could be over quickly.

She did notice that Mr. Black let his eyes slide in the direction of Mr. Red more than once and the look on his face puzzled her. It was almost as if Mr. Red was the prey, not her.

Mr. Blue seemed like someone's uncle—maybe one with a secret life. He didn't seem entirely harmless. He must've been one of the older ones who had fallen behind as she had neared the booth. Though older, Mr. Blue had an intelligent look that indicated he might be able to outsmart her if he couldn't outrun her.

Mr. Green, however, was another story. Just looking at him, Amy felt a familiar heat in her loins. *My god, can I be attracted to this man?* She colored slightly. This man was young, tall, and had the most amazing green eyes. *Aptly named,* she mused. His hair was a disheveled dark blonde mop—he looked more like a surfer than a hunter. It was a shame they had to meet under these circumstances.

Sorry, cutie, she thought, *but you're going down.*

Amy was escorted to the large table, where six place settings had been arranged. They deferred to her to choose her seat, which added to the false politeness of the evening. After she sat down, the other men scrambled to find a spot, like a grown-up version of musical chairs. She was pleased to see Mr. Green had managed to grab the chair immediately to her right. Mr. Black sat on her left.

Drinks were ordered as small talk commenced. Some men ordered bourbon, others beer. Amy was careful to limit herself to one glass of Chardonnay. She wasn't about to be slowed by drink. She hoped the men all got sloshed.

"Amy, you proved to be a formidable opponent last time. You must work out regularly," Mr. Blue was saying.

Amy thought he was looking for an edge. She wasn't about to tell him she still plays competitive volleyball and runs five miles a week. "Oh, it must be my youth, I guess. I never was all that athletic in school." *Hah, take that!*

"Huh," he responded, nonplused.

"Amy, do you have a plan in mind for tomorrow?" Mr. Black filled in smoothly.

"Um. No—not any more than I had last time," she replied.

She felt something brush her leg. Amy glanced down and saw Mr. Green's left hand rest on the edge of his thigh. His knuckles touched her leg. She knew it was no coincidence. She wondered if she should object and embarrass him in front of the others.

"Why would you agree to do this again?" Mr. Red spoke from her left, distracting her. "You know your chances of winning this time around are slim."

"Maybe I just wanted to see you guys run naked for a change."

Mr. Red colored slightly. "You know what will happen when—uh, if—you lose…"

"Don't worry," she said dryly, "I've *had* sex before." Not that she was looking forward to being raped by these four strangers.

Well, three of the four, anyway, she mused. This Mr. Green is a hunk. She could imagine what would happen if he won. Amy could picture him over her naked body, sweat dripping off his coiled muscles, grasping her upper arms, thrusting his hard cock into her again and again—

"…experience?"

"What?" Someone had been talking to her and she hardly had heard a word.

"Was it the money that made you come back—or the chance on taking part in such a primal experience?" Mr. Blue repeated.

The question stirred her emotions. When she first agreed to participate in the second hunt, she had convinced herself that money was the primary factor. Deep down, she knew that the chase excited her like she had never been excited before. Something about running through the woods, being chased, knowing that if she failed, these hard men would hold her down and fuck her like the animals they all were. It was her camp experience times ten.

Amy could feel the wetness spread along her clit. Involuntarily, she squeezed her legs together. "Primal experience? Yes, I suppose it is—but I'm in this for the money, Mr. Blue," she said. It was half true.

He seemed to read her mind. He just smiled and returned to his dinner.

"Gentlemen," Mr. Red spoke up suddenly. "I propose a change in the hunt tomorrow."

Chapter 11

Conversation ceased in the room. Five pairs of eyes focused on Dirk. Bollinger seemed particularly distressed.

"I say it's time we stopped this 'Earth games' nonsense, where every hunter wins equally," Dirk said. "What kind of a contest is that for competitors like us?"

The other four hunters stared at him silently. No one objected. They seemed willing to hear him out.

"Let's face it," Dirk continued. "If this is a sport, where's the thrill of victory? We all chase her, someone catches her and goes first, then we all dive in. If we win, we basically get the same prize."

"Now wait a minute, gentle—" Bollinger began.

Jackson cut him off. "What do you propose?" His eyes narrowed.

"I'd like to see winner-take-all."

"No—no way," Steve put in. "You have the advantage over me due to age anyway. This way, I'd stand almost no chance."

"Hear me out," Dirk said. "I've thought this through. If the girl wins, she gets a hundred grand, right? I say the first hunter to reach her gets a hundred grand—plus he's the only one who gets the girl."

"That still doesn't—" Steve cut in.

"I know, I know. I've thought about that as well. Because you're older, we'd give you the tranquilizer gun," he told Steve.

Steve opened, then closed his mouth. He sat back, his lips pursed.

Dirk looked at Amy. "But that still doesn't make it completely fair—to the prey."

Amy sat up. She hadn't really been a party to this conversation up until now. "Wh-what do you mean?"

"Mr. White has some paint pistols in that locker," Dirk pointed. "I say we give you one with, say, eight rounds. If we get painted, we're out."

Dirk could see them all thinking hard. He felt he nearly had them.

"That way," he continued. "It won't be the fastest man who wins—it will be the cleverest. It also means the contest will last longer than a lousy forty-five minutes, like the last one did."

The men said nothing as each considered Dirk's proposal. It made good sense. The contest becomes a real battle of wits, with everyone on an equal footing.

"Now, gentlemen, the rules I've develop—" Bollinger tried again.

"Can it, mister. We're thinking," said Jackson.

Amy sat stunned. From her point of view, it was a much better deal. With a weapon, she stood a far better chance of keeping the men at bay until she reached the safety booth. And if she lost, god forbid, instead of four rapes, she'd only have to face one. And one might not be so bad—if it was the right one. She glanced over at Mr. Green.

"There's one final point," Dirk added. Again, he had their full attention. "If we agree to arm the girl, then there's no need for a safety booth. To win, she'd have to paint us all."

So much for my advantage, Amy thought. "What's the range of a paint gun?" She asked.

"Twenty yards max, maybe less," Bollinger answered dully. He could see the tide turning against him.

"Well, gentlemen, what do you think?" Dirk asked finally.

"I like it," Jackson said immediately.

"If I'm getting the tranquilizer gun, then so do I," Steve piped up.

"I could go along," Jake said slowly, eyeing Amy. "But what about her?"

"I'm-I'm not sure," she said slowly. "Without the booth, I'm at a real disadvantage. My weapon has a very short range. I don't like it."

There was a silence. The men felt they were close to an agreement, they just needed something to sweeten it for the prey.

"How about this," Dirk spoke up. "The booth stays — but it's locked for the first half-hour. You survive thirty minutes, then you can head to the booth."

Thirty minutes! Could she survive a half-hour out there with these four men after her? It was a tremendous concession. She searched for flaws in the hunt.

"The rules could be hard to enforce," she said. "For example, if I get hit by a dart and I manage to paint the, uh, Mr. Blue in return, I still lose because I'll fall unconscious, but Mr. Blue can't win because he's been painted. How do we resolve issues like this?"

Dirk shrugged. "The first one who reaches you who isn't marked wins," he said. "Mr. Blue will have to be careful after he darts you." He looked around. "Agreed?"

Heads nodded.

"But without a referee right there on the scene, I can see disagreements over that," she pressed. "And I can't very well have Mr. White follow me on the cart — that would give me away."

Surprisingly, Bollinger came up with the answer. "Well, I wasn't going to do this because this was a special hunt and everyone was going to be, uh, unclothed. But we could outfit everyone with the video cameras. If there was a disagreement, we could go to the tape."

Heads began nodding all around. "Wait," put in Jake. "Are weapons transferable? In other words, if Mr. Blue here gets painted, can one of us pick up his weapon?"

Bollinger nodded. "Good point. What's the consensus?"

"Transferable," Jackson and Dirk said simultaneously. Jake nodded.

"Okay, then. Weapons can be picked up—but only to a man who's unmarked," Bollinger said. "I think we have an agreement."

"Um," Steve broke in, embarrassed. "What about the shaving part? Are we still going to do that?"

The men smiled a little at Steve's apparent fetish. "What, like second prize?" Jackson said derisively. "In a winner-take-all contest? Let the winner do that—if he wants to."

Amy reddened as the men discussed what was to become of her private parts.

"Tell ya what, Mr. Blue," Dirk put in. "Let's make that the booby prize. First one eliminated gets to shave her — after the winner is finished, of course."

There was laughter all around—and instant agreement.

"Wait—one final point," Amy jumped in before they could finalize the new deal. "The bloodhound stays home. I don't want my position given away."

"Of course," Dirk said. "Agreed?"

Everyone nodded. Even Amy thought it was more than fair. She planned to put as much distance between them and her as possible and stay hidden. Once the half-hour was up, she could look for the booth, and use the paint guns to keep them at bay. She was still at a disadvantage in weaponry, but overall, she felt she had a much better chance.

"That will change the equipment requirements, you realize," Bollinger said. "If Amy is going to be returning fire, all of you must wear goggles to prevent eye injuries."

The men weren't thrilled by the idea of wearing goggles in this heat, but they understood it was necessary.

A new agreement was drawn up and signed. Bollinger didn't like it, but he had to admit it was more because he hadn't thought of it himself. In retrospect, it was a solid plan. He made a mental note to steal the idea for himself later.

After dinner, Bollinger took Amy aside and suggested that too much familiarity might affect her chances tomorrow. She didn't disagree and slipped away as the men retired to the den to smoke and have their after-dinner brandies.

Jake caught her eye before she left. "Good luck tomorrow," he said softly. She thought he really meant it. She nodded shyly in return.

The men stayed up for awhile, swapping hunting stories and sharing jokes, drinking nightcaps until 11 p.m. They studiously avoided talking about their failed hunt of the day before, as the one tomorrow was completely different in scope and rules.

All in all, they were a very confident bunch who said their goodbyes that night.

Jake retired to his room and stripped off his clothes. He wanted to get right to sleep, so he'd be sharp tomorrow, but there was something eating at him. That woman — girl, almost — had a hold on him. He wished he had met her somewhere else. Chasing her down like a deer would probably ruin his chances of ever getting a date with her.

Duh — ya think? He snorted at himself.

Unconsciously, his hand drifted down to his cock, which was swelling even at the thought of her. He touched the shaft gently, stroking it as he let his mind wander. He could imagine a date with her easily. A quiet dinner at his favorite spot, Splash, along the waterfront, followed by some after-dinner drinks. Jake knew the chef there. He'd ask him to make up something special for them, just to impress her.

He knew they'd hit it off. Talk would come easily, as if they had been friends for years. He thought of afterwards, as he drove her home. She'd be feeling good. They'd stop outside her apartment — no, he'd want to show her his place. She'd be curious as to what a dotcom millionaire's house looked like.

His hands wrapped around his shaft as he imagined her expression when she saw his house. "Oh, my, Jake, you have excellent taste," she'd say.

"I know what I like," he'd respond, taking her hand and kissing it. She'd blush, knowing what he meant.

They'd have one more drink by the fireplace in the library. An educated woman like Amy would love the library. He'd lean in close and touch the side of her face, telling her how pretty she was. She'd smile and look down, trying to be modest.

He stroked himself harder now as he pictured himself lifting her chin to kiss her on the lips, just gently, like a butterfly's kiss. Her mouth would open to his, sucking at him hungrily. He'd kiss her hard, letting his hand come around to unzip the back of her dress. Her clothes would slip off easily.

The sight of her naked for the first time would pierce his heart. Not like on the hunt, which was crass and crude by comparison. No, she'd be willing, wanting him. He would reach down and touch her bare breast, listening to her slight intake of breath. He'd kiss her neck, let her feel his fingers tracing a light pattern down her stomach to her secret garden.

He'd gently kiss her stomach, listening to her sighs. Fingertips would dance across her heated skin. Moving lower, he'd inhale the aroma of her womanhood. It would be intoxicating, he knew.

She would be wet, of course. When his tongue first touched her, she'd arch her back and make keening sounds deep in her throat. He loved to bring pleasure to a woman this way and he'd found women really appreciated it. Not all men enjoyed oral sex—a concept he couldn't fathom.

He would bring her to her first orgasm gently, licking her, flicking her clit as she wiggled and gasped until her release took hold. He'd let her rest a few minutes, enjoying the glow.

She would want him badly now. As his hand pumped his cock, Jake imagined her hands on it, finally. Amy would have a delicate touch, as if she was unsure what to do with it. As his fingers slid along her wet slit, she would become bolder and wrap her hand around his cock and begin stroking harder.

He would press her down onto the couch. Her legs would fall open for him, giving him complete access to her core. He'd be gentle at first, easing the head of his cock between her labial lips, gazing into her eyes. When she was ready, he'd plunge in with one stroke, feeling her tight, wet cunt drawing him in. He'd begin moving back and forth, increasing the pressure on his hard cock...

With a groan, Jake came in a spurt, white cream flying over the bedsheets. His thoughts of Amy faded. Embarrassed, he grabbed a tissue and mopped up.

"Jeez, gal, I'd give you the hundred grand if you'd go out with me," he murmured. He was sure after tomorrow, she'd never want to see any of them ever again.

He sighed, the long overdue guilt settling in. He could hardly blame her.

Chapter 12

Amy was up at 6:30, nervously pacing the room. She had slipped on the dress she wore the night before, leaving the underwear on the bed. She felt more comfortable with some clothes on, at least for a while.

Bollinger came in at 7, as promised, and brought her a plate of food. He paid no attention to her dress. "Are you ready for the hunt, my dear?"

"Yes, as ready as I'm going to be." She looked at him sharply. "This contest had better be like we agreed."

"Of course, my dear. I have a reputation to maintain." He excused himself.

The group ate breakfast silently, thinking about the hunt. Truth be told, they were more worried about running naked than winning. What seemed like a good idea in the heat of the moment last night now caused acute embarrassment. Most felt like a schoolboy who had agreed to appear in a play, only to develop severe stage fright on opening night.

Three of the four men had dressed for breakfast. Only Jake, "Mr. Green," came dressed in a robe and tennis shoes. Everyone assumed he was naked under it. The other men felt he was showing off a little because he was the youngest.

Bollinger tapped his empty orange juice glass with a spoon. "Gentlemen, we're going to draw for weapons. Because of the agreement last night, we'll only be drawing for the net gun."

Jake, Jackson, and Dirk put their names in the coffee can. Bollinger picked a net gun out of the rack and held it up, then reached into the can with his free hand. "Jackson," he said.

Jake and Dirk breathed sighs of relief. Jackson, however, wasn't concerned. Now that Amy was going to have a weapon, they all had to change their plans of attack. Jackson wanted to make sure she ran out of ammunition before he moved in. The net gun wouldn't be a disadvantage. *Besides, I may end up using it on Dirk anyway,* he mused.

Bollinger passed out the bolo guns, then took out a paint pistol for Amy. He counted out eight paint balls and loaded them into the hopper. He looked at his watch. "It's 7:30. I suggest you all get undressed for the hunt and return here. We still have to outfit you with the video gear."

The men nervously retired to their rooms, except Jake, who simply dropped his robe, unabashed. "I'm ready when you are, Mr. White."

Amy was escorted out of her room about 15 minutes later. She was again naked, dressed only in her running shoes. Just before Bollinger arrived, she had looked down and said a silent goodbye to her downy hair.

Chapter 13

The men were ill at ease even before Amy walked in. They were all naked, but where they were lumpy and bumpy, she was all smooth curves. Steve turned aside, embarrassed, trying to hide his limp cock and flabby belly. The others used their guns to cover themselves. Except Jake. He just stood there, taking her in and letting her see his nakedness.

Amy laughed silently at the other men's discomfort. *Serves you right, you perverts!*

Her eyes were drawn to their limp cocks—she couldn't help herself. Mentally, she wondered if the size of their cocks had any bearing on their hunting ability. If so, Mr. Red would be the one to watch out for—his soft penis hung down a good two inches beyond the others. Mr. Black's cock was above average, staying true to the stereotype she'd heard about black men's big dicks. Mr. Blue's was all shriveled and surrounded by gray-white hair. *Ewww!* Mr. Green's, she was pleased to see, was a close second to Mr. Red's. For the briefest second, she imagined it sliding into her.

She shook her head to clear the image and scolded herself. *You have work to do, Miss Dellacroix!*

They had to stand quietly while Bollinger strapped the video gear on them. It consisted of a small video camera the size of the cap to a cheap pen attached by cable to a fanny pack containing the battery and the transmitter. Each signal would be transmitted to a separate video recorder in the main house.

Bollinger ran the cable up between their shoulder blades to baseball caps on everyone's head. Amy wrapped her hair up and tucked it underneath her cap.

She couldn't help but notice a few minutes later, when Mr. White silently handed each man a flat foil packet—condoms. They slipped them into the fanny packs, keeping their eyes averted from her.

Bollinger passed out sunscreen and urged everyone to slather it on. "You might be out there for hours, you never know," he said.

"Hah! You white boys shore look like you could use it," Jackson laughed.

Reluctantly, the other men passed around the tube, keeping their eyes on Amy as she rubbed the liquid onto her shoulders, breasts and the rounded curve of her ass.

"Want some help?" She turned to see Mr. Green standing there, nodding at the tube she held in her hand.

Amy blushed. "Um, just on my back, okay?" He took the tube from her. All the other men eyed him with envy. Jake rubbed it into her shoulders, moving down her back to the soft curve of her ass.

She reached down and lightly touched his hand. "Careful," she said. "I think I can take if from here." The other men snickered.

Amy tried to hide it, but she could feel herself growing wet. She wasn't sure if it was Mr. Green or the upcoming chase. Her attraction to the man was physical, yes, but there was something primal about this hunt that affected her as well. It seemed to go beyond her memories of camp. Perhaps they were reverting to the caveman in all of us, she mused. Was that how it was for a female Neanderthal? Getting chased down by the strongest man in the tribe, then dragged off to be mated? It probably was. Now history may repeat itself.

By 8:05, they were ready to go. Amy led them out on the porch this time, unwilling to act the part of the victim. She cradled the paint gun against her left forearm. The men trailed behind, getting a good look at the firm globes of her ass. Three of the men wished they were ten years younger again.

Bollinger passed out the goggles. "Gentlemen—and lady—you've all agreed to the new rules. My assistant left earlier this morning in a cart to secure the booth. He will listen for my shot, telling him that Amy's five-minute head start has begun. He will check his watch and exactly thirty minutes later, he'll unlock the booth and start returning to the lodge. He won't fire immediately, however. That's so he won't give away the exact position of the booth. Once he's safely away, he'll fire two blasts of his shotgun, letting you know the booth is open.

"Amy, after you've started, I'll wait five minutes, then fire two shots to let you know that the men have been released. Gentlemen, if the prey is captured or if she reaches the booth, I'll fire three shots to let the rest of you know the game is over. Is everybody ready?"

The men nodded, hanging back under the porch. Amy stood near the front steps, again visualizing the sweep of property before her. One booth. It could be anywhere. If she guessed wrong, she probably would lose. Last time she went south and found one. Is the only booth north this time? She debated.

Behind her, Bollinger raised the pistol. "GO!" he shouted, simultaneously firing a shot into the air. The noise again galvanized Amy into action. She jumped off the porch and cut left, heading straight down the gravel road toward the gate.

All eyes watched her until she ran around a corner out of sight behind the row of trees, her athletic body making the men ache with desire.

"Four minutes, thirty seconds," Bollinger said.

Chapter 14

Amy ran straight for the gate. She hoped that by running along the well-worn road, she might add a few precious yards between her and her pursuers. She had nearly three miles to the gate.

Amy had a crude plan—she didn't even know if it would work. She wanted to find the booth, then look for a place to hide for thirty minutes, paint gun or no paint gun. She knew that if she got into a showdown with the four armed men, she would lose. Mr. Blue, for one, could just stand off 50 yards and pick her off with his long gun.

When she was a half-mile away from the lodge, she turned south, making a large looping turn 180 degrees back. She wanted to come in well behind the lodge going east just as the men were heading in the opposite direction on her false trail. Then, she'd continue east until she neared the fence. At that point, she'd have to decide—north or south?

"Two minutes, gentlemen."

The men on the porch were agitated now, ready to go. They gathered near the steps, their nudity forgotten as they visualized the running woman in their minds. They gripped their guns tighter. Everyone was thinking about winning and what that would mean to him.

To Steve, it would show that he still has what it takes, even though he's much older then the other men. To Dirk, it would vindicate his suggestion that they change the rules. Winner-take-all was much more appealing to him. To Jake, it meant he would be able to have his girl. The money was secondary. He saw the way she had looked at him.

Only Jackson had an ulterior motive today. He still burned over Dirk's "accidental" shooting, just as he was about to claim his prize. He knew it was no accident. Jackson wanted the girl, sure, and the money—but what he really wanted was to see Dirk go down in defeat. If he needed a push, he'd be happy to provide it.

"One minute," Bollinger said.

Amy's breath came in gasps. She had tried to cover too much ground too fast, she realized—and now she was almost back where she started. From her position, she couldn't see the gravel road through the line of trees, but she thought she might be able to hear them pounding along it. She knew the gunshots would be coming any second now.

There were plenty of bushes and trees to cover her position, although there were also plenty of gaps. She would have to be careful not to be spotted. She jogged on. Ahead, through the trees to the northeast, she spotted the lodge. She slowed now, conserving her strength, waiting for the men to be released.

"GO!" Bollinger shouted, firing the pistol in the air twice. The shots echoed over the property. The men all jumped off the porch and gave chase, heading west down the gravel road. Only Steve hung behind, already trying to conserve his energy.

Amy heard the shots clearly, then hunkered down behind a large tree. She knew she should keep running, but she was afraid someone would catch a glimpse of her. Her plan would be ruined then.

She didn't have to wait long. The pounding of feet alerted her and she hid, breathing hard, trying not to panic. She risked a peek through a gap in the bushes and spotted Mr. Red jogging by, his dick flapping as he ran. Right behind him came Mr. Black, then Mr. Green, and finally, Mr. Blue, holding the tranquilizer gun across his chest. Amy ducked again and waited until the pounding of feet passed by.

She got up and ran.

Chapter 15

Roger Bollinger turned on five of the seven TVs in the den and watched the shaky images. Unbeknownst to the participants, he had placed grid markings at regular intervals on the trees throughout the property. Any time a grid marker showed up on a screen, he knew instantly where that person's location was.

He was shocked, therefore, to see Amy's camera pick up the marker 2E-2S when she should've been much farther west. The prey had turned around! He smiled. "You go, girl."

He left the den and climbed the stairs to the second-floor loft. It had picture windows all around. Picking up a pair of binoculars, he focused it southeast of the lodge.

There! He got a glimpse of Amy running through the trees behind the lodge, heading toward the eastern fence. She looked like a graceful animal, he thought. Fast, smart—and now, thanks to Dirk, armed. This might be the best hunt yet.

Jake followed Dirk and Jackson, but he was troubled. He looked behind him to see Steve bringing up the rear. This didn't make sense to him, all of them following the same path. Even if they found her, they'd all be bunched together, fighting for the first shot. The problem was, of course, they didn't know which direction she would ultimately go—north or south?

Well, he thought, even as he slowed further, two days ago, she went south. Maybe this time, she'll go north. He wished he knew where the booth was. Jake wondered what Andy would do if he were here.

"Jake," he'd probably say, "it's like binary code. It's either off or on, white or black. Just pick one and go."

When Steve jogged past him, breathing hard, Jake cut right—to the north.

Amy felt she had run about a mile and a half east, well past the lodge. She didn't want to wait until she saw the fence this time, she had to make her move now. North or south, north or south? *Where's that goddammed booth?*

Hell, it was south last time, maybe Bollinger put it north. Or maybe he'd figure she'd think it was north, so he put it south. *Dammit!*

Amy swung northward.

Dirk, jogging just a few steps in front of Jackson, turned to see how far back the other two men were and was surprised not to see Jake. He slowed and Jackson slowed as well, grateful for the break. He was winded. *Shit!* Back in his day, he could do two-a-day workouts without a thought, or run the length of the field like the wind.

"Jake's gone," Dirk said. Jackson turned. Sure enough, only Steve was jogging along behind them. He caught up quickly.

"He...cut...north," Steve said, gasping between words.

"He's probably right," Dirk said. "We should split up, otherwise, we'll be all over each other."

"I'll go south," Steve volunteered, happy to leave these hyper-competitive men who reminded him just how much of his youth he had lost.

"Yeah," Dirk said. "We're still about a mile and a half away from the fence. I'll go to the end and cut north. You wanna go to the end and go south?" He looked at Jackson.

Jackson just grinned, showing a lot of white teeth. "Nah. I'll stick with you for a while."

Dirk didn't like the sound of that. *He must still be pissed about the dart.* Suddenly, he realized Jackson could make it hard for him to win this contest. He eyed the net gun warily.

"Maybe we shouldn't split up, after all," he said. "Steve's got the long gun—we could really use that."

"You got the bolo—you still got a longer range than the girl," Jackson noted. Until this moment, he didn't realize just how much he wanted to be alone with Dirk. He could feel his muscles rippling with anger along his back.

"Hey, it's every man for himself. I'm going south," Steve announced and without waiting for argument, he jogged off.

"Shit," Dirk said. "I hope we don't need that."

"Why? You hoping to get a hold of it again?"

Dirk shook his head. "Come on, we're wasting time." They continued down the road.

Chapter 16

The men were scattered now, except for Dirk and Jackson. Bollinger caught glimpses of grid locations in the five screens, then closed his eyes, visualizing the layout of the playing field. He wanted to be ready when the hunters closed in on their prey. He could see it all: Jake running north, Steve running south, Dirk and Jackson still running west along the road.

The prey was running north as well, not far from the eastern fence.

He smiled. The safety booth had been placed south again this time. In fact, he told Mort not to bother moving it, only to collect the one in the north and bring it back to the barn. The girl had no chance now.

He looked back at the screen. "You're going in the wrong direction, honey," he breathed.

Amy was thoroughly winded. She guessed she was still a good mile or more from the north fence. She hoped she had guessed right, otherwise this would be a short contest. The gun was heavy in her hand and she almost wished she hadn't been given the nearly useless weapon. Amy felt like she had been running for an hour, yet it was probably less than twenty minutes.

Jake jogged on, tired but wary, trying to listen for footsteps or other noises through the trees. He guessed he was nearing the north fence now. He slowed and began to drift east. Because all three men were running west, he didn't want to get near them again. They may well have her already, he thought angrily. Then again, he hadn't heard any shots from Bollinger's gun.

Steve felt like the loneliest man on the planet. The farther he ran, the more he was convinced he had gone the wrong way.

Still, he knew he had to cover the ground. He was really tired and the thorns scratched his naked flesh as he ran by them. *This wasn't such a good idea*, he thought. *I should've admitted I was too old for this.*

That would make Phil right, he realized. He was determined not to admit that to himself.

Jackson had a very simple plan in mind for Dirk. He'd let him get close to Amy, then tangle him up with the net. He hoped the girl would be out of ammo by then. If not, he might have to dodge and weave until she was. Then he would simply tackle her, like he had so many running backs and wide receivers.

Dirk was trying to figure out how to shake Jackson. He knew the man was out to spoil his fun. Dirk also knew he probably deserved it. What had been a wild, spur-of-the-moment decision in the earlier hunt could easily end up costing him one hundred grand. *Maybe I should shoot him first*, he thought.

Chapter 17

Amy had to rest. She was breathing so hard, she thought she might pass out. *Perhaps I should change my strategy. Rest now and look for the booth when it opens.* She knew that was her weakness talking. She had no use for it today. Not if she wanted to win this.

Amy forced herself on. She wasn't running any longer, just loping or walking fast, breathing in great gasps. Sweat poured off her body and got in her eyes. She grabbed some leaves from a tree and tried to wipe down her forehead, only to have more sweat replace it.

She was about to come out of a copse of trees into a meadow when instinct made her stop and crouch down. A noise froze her. *There!* A man was skirting the edge of the meadow about two hundred yards to her left. Amy squinted. It was Mr. Green, the handsome one. Her stomach flip-flopped and the heat extended down to her loins. Being naked only exacerbated her lust. Her imagination flashed on an image of her, down on the ground, her legs spread wide, as Mr. Green thrust into her again and again.

She shook off the thought. *What the hell's wrong with me?* Amy watched him move north, letting him go, for now. Her predatory feelings surprised her. She fought to concentrate on her strategy. Now he was between her and the fence. If the booth was up there, he could just wait nearby until she showed up. *Dammit!* Her narrow odds just got longer.

Steve's luck was incredible. He had gone straight south from the road, leaving everyone behind. Now, through the trees ahead, he spotted the telltale red splash of color. *The booth!* He jogged closer, trying to keep out of sight in case the woman was already here.

When he was within two hundred yards, he spotted Mort standing by his cart. Steve guessed they had about another ten minutes before the booth would be opened. He didn't see Amy anywhere. Of course, she could be keeping herself well hidden. Steve crept the last hundred yards, staying out of sight. If he could hide himself in front here, Amy may not see him until it was too late. He could dart her, then grab her when the drug took effect.

Steve settled down to wait.

Chapter 18

Amy followed Mr. Green, keeping well back. By now, she was beginning to doubt she had gone in the right direction. Still, she had to be sure. If she kept the hunter in her line of sight, and watched carefully behind her as well, she should be able to determine if the booth was placed along the northern fence or not. She'd pause now and then, checking behind her in a slow circle, to make sure no one was sneaking up on her.

Suddenly, a full-throated shot rang through the air, followed by another one. Both came from behind her. She whirled around, angrily.

Shit! I'd guessed wrong after all. Amy knew at that moment that she'd never be allowed to reach the booth now. By the time she got there, it would be well-guarded. The hunters would just hang around and wait her out. No doubt they were all running toward the noise—except Mr. Green.

Amy hunkered down in the bushes and soon caught sight of her opponent jogging south. He would be coming very close, she noticed. An idea took hold of her. She struggled with it.

She hid behind a tree as Mr. Green approached. When she heard his footsteps clearly, she jumped out, raised her gun and shouted, "Freeze!"

Jake was so startled, he dropped his gun as he whirled around. He stood, mouth agape, then grimaced and closed his eyes, waiting for the inevitable splat of color that would put him out of the game. It never came.

Cautiously, he opened his eyes again. The girl was just standing there in her glorious nakedness, breathing hard and watching him, the gun aimed squarely on his chest. He could feel his cock harden.

He started to speak, then stopped. Words did not seem important now. Tentatively, he took a step toward her, away from his gun lying in the dirt. She kept her gun steady on his chest.

His cock ached. He felt it leading him on. He sensed she felt the same way.

Amy was confused. She had meant to surprise him, then shoot him and knock him out of the hunt. Yet she stood here, watching him, unable to move. Something powerful was happening. Her cunt was leaking, the juices covering her clit. A strange heat emanated from her loins.

She opened her mouth, then closed it again. There was nothing to say. She took a step forward, her gun beginning to droop. He followed, closing the gap between them.

They were just five yards apart now, eyes burning into each other's. Amy's breath caught in her throat. It was as if all the normal rules had been suspended. They were naked, they were hunter and hunted — only which was which? It would have been easy to resist their mutual attraction in more conventional setting. But here, now…

Her gun dropped to the ground; they rushed to close the gap between them. She felt his hot breath on her lips, then his mouth smothered hers, his arms enveloped her. Her breasts were pressed tightly between them, sweat mingling.

Jake felt his hard cock press against her stomach. Her incredible warmth made him harder still. He had to have her.

The bills of their caps bumped and suddenly, both realized that they were being recorded! With hardly a pause, they ripped off their hats and wrapped the material around the lenses. They looked at each other and smiled.

Stripping off the fanny packs, they both took a few seconds to scan the horizon. They were alone. Motioning to her, Jake led her to a group of bushes. Behind them, there was some meadow grass, protected from the sun.

They dropped their packs, making sure the cameras remained blinded. They fell together onto the grass.

At the lodge, Bollinger stared at the two dark screens. He stopped the tape and backed it up, not believing what he had just seen. The look of lust in the eyes of those two was unmistakable. The way they came together, the images blurring as they met, made him hard. He adjusted his pants, then opened the top drawer of his desk and pulled out the contract. He began reading.

Amy wanted Jake, needed him, had to have him. His mouth fastened on her breast; she hugged him to her, humping her groin against his thigh. He reached down and touched her cunt — she nearly had an orgasm right then and there.

Jake kissed her again, tasting her sweet scent. He lost himself in her: mouth, neck, breasts, arms, legs — and hot, wet cunt. There was more animal than girl in her. The inside of her thighs were soaked, he felt it coat his fingers.

Without a word, he moved between her legs. She opened herself immediately, then grabbed him around the neck. His hard cock found its mark. Jake poised there, relishing the best moment of a man's life — about to plunge into the slippery core of a willing woman.

In one motion, he was fully inside her. She gasped and made inarticulate noises in her throat. Amy wrapped her legs around his waist and hung on as Jake began to thrust deep into her. Colors ran together; she closed her eyes and saw stars.

The orgasm was building, building, timed with the noises of their union — the slap of their thighs, the wet sounds of cock and cunt, the soft moans of desire. Their world was reduced to this moment in time.

Their timing, incredibly, was perfect. Just as Jake erupted in a hoarse cry, Amy shook with an orgasm that seemed to race from her curled toes to the top of her head. She felt his hot sperm flood her womb. They clung together, unwilling to let the blissful encounter end. It was, by far, the best orgasm she had ever experienced.

Too late, she remembered the condom in his fanny pack. In the heat of the moment, it hadn't mattered. Idly, almost with detachment, she wondered if she was pregnant.

Finally, they separated and lay, exhausted, staring up at the brilliant blue sky.

"I thought you were going to shoot me," he panted. It was the first words they had spoken to each other today.

She laughed. "I was planning to. But there was something about seeing you standing there, naked, with your cock growing hard, that made me change my mind. I guess this means you've won. After all," she rolled over and touched his chest, "you've already claimed your prize."

He thought about that. Yes, it was true—he had gotten to her first. But it wasn't right. She had let him win. She had him dead to rights. He'd been outplayed.

"No," he said. He knew that somehow Bollinger would know. And he'd never let this pass. He sighed, trying to figure out what to do. "It isn't right. Bollinger won't buy it. I didn't earn it."

Amy didn't say anything for a minute. Then: "So what do we do now?"

He turned to her. "Let's pretend, for the purposes of the game, that this never happened. You had me in your sights, so you shoot me and go try to win this game—and the hundred grand." He stilled. "In exchange, maybe you'd agree to go to dinner with me sometime?"

"That's very fair of you. But I don't want you out of the game quite yet," she said. "But, then again, I don't want to lose to any other man." The thought of having any one of the other three men root with her on the ground would spoil her memory of her encounter with Jake.

"Well, if this never happened, then I guess I'm not out of the game, either."

She sat up. "So we'd just go on as before? You hunting me down like the rest?"

"Hmm. Not quite. I wouldn't really be trying to make you lose after all. You could think of me as your safety valve, you know. If it looked like you were going to lose, I could get you first." He grinned. "You deserve that hundred grand."

Amy's cheeks dimpled with her smile. "A man among beasts," she whispered.

They got up and put their gear back on, dusting off the dirt and grass stains as best as they could. They returned to where their weapons lay. She bent down to pick up the paint gun and his bolo gun.

"Since you're not going to be hunting, you won't need this," She slung his gun over her shoulder. "Consider yourself disarmed."

"Okay, pad'ner, you gots me." Jake raised his hands in mock surrender.

They stared at each other like two cowboys on a dusty street in Tombstone. Then their eyes began to drift down to their bodies and determination gave way to renewed lust. Jake felt himself getting hard again. They both chuckled.

"By the way, my name is Jake," he said.

"You already know I'm Amy."

He glanced away, nervously clearing his throat. "Maybe after this is over, we could, hmm, see each other?" he said quietly. He turned his gaze back to her, his eyes hopeful. And a bit vulnerable.

A sudden noise distracted them.

Chapter 19

"What the hell is this?" Dirk said, hiding behind a bush, Jackson close beside him.

They peered out to see their prey talking to Jake. They watched as she bent down and scooped up his weapon. They could also see his erection from one hundred yards away. Jake raised his hands.

"What's she doing?" Jackson asked. "Making a deal?"

"Either that or flirting. Maybe she shot him already and we can't see from here."

"If she did, he still wouldn't have his hands raised. No, there's some funny business going on."

"Come on. Maybe we can sneak up on her while she's distracted."

"Shee-it. How could she be distracted by that little white-boy dick?"

"Jake'll be able to see us, you know. We should split up," Dirk said. "You approach her from the side, I'll come at her from behind. When she bolts, I'll bolo her legs."

"And while I'm being the diversion, who gets to claim her? Jake or you?" Jackson sneered.

Dirk let his anger flash. "Look, Jackson, having you hang around with me isn't doing either of us any good. It's winner-take-all, remember? That means I don't need a teammate."

Jackson paused, then looked across the one hundred yards that separated him from victory — and one hundred grand. Back in his playing days, he could run the hundred-yard dash in twelve seconds. Now, it'd probably take him fifteen. He wondered how fast Amy could run.

"All right," he said, turning to Dirk. "Start swinging around behind her. I'll wait a few minutes, then charge her."

Dirk eyed him cautiously, surprised that he suddenly agreed with his plan. Then he nodded and got up in a half-crouch and began to move north. Jackson let him get about ten yards away before he raised his net gun at Dirk's retreating back and fired. The net gun made a "whoomp" as it exploded from the gun.

The net puffed out just as Dirk turned back toward him, his eyes wide and uncomprehending. The net wrapped around him and dropped him to the ground. In an instant, Jackson, threw away his weapon and was up and running full-tilt toward the startled woman.

Amy and Jake heard the sound of the gun and turned in time to see the black man bursting from the undergrowth, running right at them. Amy screamed and started to run.

"Shoot him!" Jake shouted, seeing at once that Jackson didn't have his gun.

Amy was in full panic mode, her legs churning as she ran past Jake toward the southwest, trying to put some distance between her and the hunter.

Jake's shout caused her to look over her shoulder. She watched as Jake threw himself in the path of the charging Mr. Black. The action startled the big man. He tried to sidestep him, but his aging muscles failed him and they collided. Both men went down in a heap.

Jackson jumped up, enraged at the interference, conveniently forgetting that he had just cheated Dirk out of his chance. He grabbed Jake by the neck and hauled him to his feet, the hunt forgotten for a moment. "You mother-fucker!" he screamed, his face a mask of hatred. He drew back his hand and punched Jake hard in the jaw. The man went down.

Jackson reached down and hauled Jake up again when he heard a "plop" sound and felt something slap him between the shoulder blades. A wetness ran down, mixing with his sweat.

"You're out, asshole. Now leave him alone." He dropped Jake, and turned to see Amy standing there with her paintgun raised. He looked over his shoulder at the bright purple paint dripping down his broad back.

"Maybe I'll just take my prize anyway, bitch," he said, still seething.

"Run, Amy!" Jake shouted from the ground and grabbed Jackson around the legs.

She turned and ran, completely on adrenaline, her fear driving her on. Jake's gun banged painfully into her back. Amy knew she was abandoning Jake to an uncertain fate, but she couldn't stay there with that madman Mr. Black. Heck with the hunt—she was now in fear for her life.

Chapter 20

Back at the lodge, Bollinger sat bolt upright when the new images appeared on the screens. It was one thing to watch Jake and Amy making some kind of deal, but when Jackson ran up and collided with Jake, then began punching him, he had to stop them.

He ran out and jumped into his cart and sped off toward the grid where the men were fighting. He caught a brief glimpse of Amy running south, crying, about two hundred yards away. Bollinger jerked the wheel as he dodged trees, trying to get to the two men before one was seriously hurt. Unconsciously, his right hand dropped down to touch his pistol.

When Jake grabbed Jackson and hung on, he knew he was in for a beating from the stronger man. Still, he had to give Amy at least a little head start. Jackson struggled violently and he fell down next to Jake. He managed to free one leg and kicked at Jake's head, causing him to release his grip.

Jake groaned and rolled away, feeling a lump form on his forehead. He looked up in time to see Jackson spring to his feet and turn south.

Before he could take a step, however, a blur appeared over Jake's head and tackled Jackson, knocking him back to the ground. *It's Dirk!* Jake realized. Both men writhed around on the ground. Jake scooted away, listening to their curses.

"You bastard! You cheated! You were waiting for that all day!"

"You started it, you pussy! I had her the other day and you shot me!"

"It was an accident!"

"Bullshit! You don't expect me to believe that!"

Both men struggled to their feet and began swinging wildly at each other. Jackson was more powerful, but Dirk had a few tricks of his own. He stepped inside of Jackson's punches and grabbed him. In seconds, they had fallen down again, legs and arms pinwheeling.

Jake, shaking his head, crawled away, then got up and began slowly jogging south, trying to follow Amy's path.

When Bollinger pulled up a few minutes later, he found the two naked hunters grappling on the ground. Sighing, he pulled out his pistol and fired a round into the air. "You're supposed to be fucking the girl, not each other," he said dryly.

Both men stopped and separated, looking up sheepishly at the referee, then down at their nakedness. They had exhausted themselves in the heat and Bollinger's words brought them back to reality.

"I'm lodging a protest!" Dirk said as he struggled to his feet. "This man turned his net gun on me!"

"You shot me first the other day! Be a man and admit it!" Jackson said.

Dirk couldn't admit it, not even to himself. He started to speak, then snapped his mouth closed.

"I knew it, you fucking cheater! When it happens to you, you don't like it much, do you?"

Dirk didn't say anything. He was too embarrassed to speak. His eyes slid around, unwilling to catch the eyes of either man.

"Well, you gentlemen can protest all you want, but that won't change the winner-takes-all nature of this hunt," Bollinger said. "It appears you are out, Mr. Black. But you, Mr. Red, are untouched. Unless you want to quit and return with me to file your 'protest,' I suggest you keep playing."

Dirk realized he had wasted a lot of time. "Yeah," he said, and turned to retrieve his weapon and his goggles, which had fallen off in the struggle. Without another word, he jogged south, after Amy.

"I want to protest Jake—Mr. Green," Jackson said, unwilling to accept that he had been eliminated. "He knocked me down, just as I was about to capture the girl. I think they made some kind of deal."

"Yes, I saw that on the video." Bollinger didn't tell him that wasn't all he observed. "But you guys made up these new rules. And there's nothing in there that says the prey can't make a deal with a hunter, repugnant as it may be. Now if you'd all agreed to stick to my rules, this never would have happened."

"Ahh, fuck you," Jackson said, walking past him toward the lodge, knowing that further argument would be futile. Twice in two hunts he had been in position to win, only to be thwarted by cheaters.

"Want a ride?"

"No, I'd rather walk."

Bollinger watched as the big man strode away into the bushes.

Chapter 21

Just one man to go, Amy thought as she jogged slowly past the lodge. It was hard to get back into the game after her passionate encounter with Jake. Juices flowed freely down the insides of her legs. Sweat was burning her eyes and sheeting off her naked body, but she kept up a steady pace. She had to find Mr. Blue before he could spot her.

She figured he would be near the safety booth, waiting for her. She hoped to sneak up behind him and put him out of business before he could shoot her.

Amy slowed as she neared the southern boundary. She stopped, placing her hands on her knees for a few minutes, trying to retain her breath. Finally, she was able to move again. She walked west. The booth had to be here somewhere.

At a large oak tree near the fence, she paused, then looked up into the branches. If she could spot the booth, she'd have a better idea of where Mr. Blue might be hiding, she decided. Carefully, she crept up into the tree, higher and higher.

Amy came to a gap in the branches that faced west and peered through. She wasn't sure, but there appeared to be a splash of color among the other trees about three hundred yards ahead. Satisfied, she came down, then began circling to the northwest, trying to get behind Mr. Blue.

Jake was beat. Like Amy, he thought only Steve remained. He didn't feel a bit guilty about interfering with Jackson because it had been instinctive when he saw him running at Amy. He felt protective of her. He hated the idea of another man touching her.

But now all he could do was wait. And hope he would be nearby if she faltered, so he could be there first.

Behind him by a good mile came Dirk, hot, dusty, embarrassed — and determined to win. This hunt had been his idea and he nearly blew it, fighting with Jackson. He had to admit that Jackson was right — he had cheated. He supposed he'd had it coming.

Though he was nearly out of the hunt, he could still win it — if he hurried. He picked up his pace.

Amy crouched down, debating. Should I try to find Mr. Blue or wait for Jake? He might be able to distract the man with the tranquilizer gun long enough for her to get into the booth.

She decided not to wait. It was too risky. Let's get this over with. She crept forward, scanning the bushes for Mr. Blue. Amy kept circling, knowing that Mr. Blue had to be around here somewhere. Where else would he be? Even if he had gone north, he would've turned around as soon as he heard the shots. No, he had to be lying in wait.

Steve, his muscles aching from his half-crouch, remained hidden in an ideal blind with bushes on three sides. He planned to wait until he heard the girl approach, then jump out and dart her. A buzzing in his ear distracted him. Unconsciously, he slapped it away.

Amy, her ears alert, heard the slap of fingers on flesh. There! She spotted a heavy growth of bushes and made a wide berth around it, so she could creep up behind him, Indian style.

Amy eased Jake's bolo gun off her shoulder. She hooked the strap of the paint gun around her neck so it hung between her breasts down to her stomach. The strap tickled her nipples. She wanted the bolo because it had a longer range. Mr. Blue wouldn't be expecting it.

She eased forward. She knew she had to get Mr. Blue out away from the bushes or the bolo would have no effect. Thinking quickly, she came up with a plan.

She crept up to within fifty yards of the hidden man — just about the range she'd need. Then, drawing in a deep breath, Amy tucked the bolo gun behind her left leg and began jogging through the bushes, making as much noise as possible and headed at an angle away from his position.

Steve was startled to hear the girl coming from almost directly behind him. He broke free of his hiding place and aimed, anticipating an easy strike. He was shocked when she ducked and whirled suddenly, brought up a bolo gun and fired back at him. He heard a whirling sound and saw the balls hurtling toward him.

Where did she get that gun!?

He tried to jump out of the way, but the strings yanked his feet together and dropped him to the ground.

The girl shouted with glee, dropped the gun and started to run. With his legs caught, Steve had just one chance to slow her down before she was out of range. From his prone position, he brought the gun around, aimed at her retreating back and pulled the trigger.

The dart hit one of the perfect globes of her ass. He silently cheered and quickly began to extricate himself from the bolo. He still had a chance!

Amy felt the dart strike her and cursed. How could he shoot me so easily? Immediately, she brushed it away, but the damage had been done. The drug swept into her bloodstream. Her legs slowed, her limbs became uncoordinated.

Amy stumbled for the booth. It was about seventy-five yards away. She could feel victory in her grasp, if she could just fight off the effects of the dart for a few more minutes.

She slipped to one knee, then forced herself to get up. She tried to remember what Mr. White had said about the darts— they were meant to slow you down, not to knock you out. The effects lasted just a half-hour or so. She willed herself to go on.

"Go for it, Amy!" She heard a voice and knew it was Jake. She waved and staggered on.

Jake watched his girl from a distance, wishing he could help her to the booth. She deserved the money. He thought she would make it and was startled to see a blur jog past him. Dirk!

"Too bad you lost your little gun," he said as he ran past.

Jake stood there stupidly. He thought the man was out of the game. "Amy! Look out!" he shouted, as Dirk quickly closed the gap. He ran to catch up.

Amy turned again, her eyes wide. No! Not Mr. Red! She could see his large cock twitch in anticipation of her capture. Her arms and legs were like rubber. She couldn't escape as Dirk fired his bolo at her legs. In seconds, she found herself on the ground.

"I got you this time!" he shouted.

Jake felt helpless. Dirk was well ahead of him, and he'd promised Amy he'd get there first. He ran faster, trying to think of some way to stop him. Preferably without cheating so Dirk wouldn't have grounds to call for another match.

Amy, lying on the ground on her back, forced her thick fingers around the butt of her paint gun. She waited for Mr. Red to approach.

Dirk was being careful this time. He remembered her bashing him with a rock. But she looked out of it now. He eased forward.

When she saw him swim into her vision, she used the last of her strength to bring up the gun and fire—one, two, three, four, five.

Dirk jerked back, startled by the sudden onslaught. Dammit! The paint gun was my idea too! He cursed himself for being careless, so late in the game. He dodged left, then right, backing up to get away from the paintballs. He backed right into Jake, who wasn't expecting Dirk's actions.

"Hey!"

Splat! An orange paintball splattered over Dirk's left arm.

"You're out," Amy breathed. She rolled over and began crawling toward the booth, the paint gun still dangling from her neck.

"You interfered with me!" Dirk bellowed. "I had her!"

"Oh, shut up." Jake rolled his eyes. "You ran into me. It's over," he panted. "She's won."

"Not quite," came a voice from behind them. Both men turned to see Steve, pulling the last of his cords from around his legs and getting to his feet. "As you gentlemen can see, I'm unmarked." He jogged toward the crawling form, ready to claim his prize.

"Amy!"

"Shut up! You can't help her. That's cheating," Dirk said.

Jake dove forward ahead of Steve and managed to get his hand on her bare leg. "I claim you!" he shouted.

Steve jumped at nearly the same time and grabbed her thigh. "No, I claim her! I shot her, I've won!"

"You're all bastards," Amy said and passed out.

Chapter 22

Three dejected men sat in Bollinger's office, watching a replay of the videos. The fourth was smiling. Amy, now recovered, sat off to one side, sipping a mineral water. Everyone was dressed.

"Want to see it again?" Bollinger asked. The cameras on Jake's and Steve's hats recorded a jumpy blur, but the camera on Dirk's head clearly showed Jake had reached the girl a second before Steve did.

"No, I've seen enough," Steve said. "But the game was rigged. Those two made a deal — you saw it."

"As I told Mr. Black here, under the rules you made up, there was no prohibition against a 'deal.' That was spelled out in the original contract, you see. Perhaps if we had stuck to those rules…"

"Aww, can it," Dirk said. Turning to Amy, he asked, "So how much did you agree to give him? Twenty percent?"

Amy colored slightly. She wasn't about to tell them what really had gone on. "No, nothing was said about money," she said truthfully. In fact, not much was said at all.

"Well, are you going to fuck her or what?" Jackson asked Jake.

Both Jake and Steve had tried to claim Amy, delaying any resolution of the hunt until Bollinger showed up to take control of the situation. Jake was not about to rape her in the dirt in front of the other men and he certainly wouldn't do it now, after their intimate encounter. He felt protective of her.

"No. Not right now. I'm out of the mood." *Actually, I feel pretty good!*

The other men snorted in disgust. They had expected to see a good fucking. Jake's response proved to them a deal had been made. Still, there was little they could do about it. For the first time, they regretted not sticking to the original rules. Had Jake passed, Steve would be next in line, followed by Dirk and Jackson.

Jackson suddenly snapped his fingers. "Wait a minute. I claim the booby prize."

All eyes swiveled towards him. "Remember the contract? The first one knocked out gets to shave her. Well, I claim that right."

Amy shook her head. "Oh, no. Not after all this. The moment's passed, bucko."

Bollinger fished the contract out of the desk and began reading. " 'The first hunter eliminated reserves the right to take the prey's pelt after the winner enjoys his sexual prize.' It's pretty clear, Amy."

"It says 'after' the winner claims his prize. I haven't claimed it yet," Jake lied.

"You gave her a pass. So I claim my rights," Jackson said.

"He has a point, Mr. Green," Bollinger said.

"All right. I'm not giving her a pass. But I'm not taking it now, either."

"You can't do that! Either put up or shut up!" Jackson retorted.

"He's right!" Dirk put in. He was surprised to find himself on Jackson's side after the bitterness between them. Maybe he was making up for that first dart in the back. Jackson gave him a wide-eyed look.

"Yeah, I agree—and it was my idea," pointed out Steve. *Hell, if I can't do it myself, at least I can watch.*

Jake looked around the group, trying to think of a way out of this. Nothing came to mind. The moment stretched out. Eyes slid over toward Amy.

"All right," Amy sighed. "You can have your jollies, Mr. Black. Just don't you dare cut me."

Jackson smiled as the other two hunters hooted. Jake looked disgusted. "Oh, I won't, Miss Amy, I won't."

The shaving gear was brought out. Amy eased up her dress and lay down on the couch. She wore no panties—she couldn't bear to have them on for a third day. She stared at the ceiling while Jackson crouched down between her legs. Tears leaked from the corners of her eyes.

All the sexual excitement she had experienced during the hunt was gone now. Amy felt like a slab of meat, laid out for the sexual gratification of these men—well, three of them anyway. She glanced at Jake, and noticed he had turned his head from the scene. She was grateful for that, at least.

"Jackson," Jake's voice froze the black man. "I'll pay you ten thousand dollars if you forego this little ritual."

Jackson looked up from between Amy's widespread legs. "Huh," he said, pursing his lips. "You know I'm worth millions, just like you," he said finally, still holding the shaving cream can in one hand.

"I know." Jake waited.

Jackson glanced down at Amy's sparse blond hair covering her mound, then up at the woman's tear-streaked face. Suddenly he felt a little ashamed of himself. This had been Steve's fetish, not his. Ten grand made his decision easier. "All right—but it's gotta be in cash."

"Jeez, I don't have ten grand on me right now, Ja—I mean, Mr. Black."

"Well, then," he smiled and squirted a dollop of shaving cream into his hand. "That's it, isn't it?"

"I have the cash," Amy said suddenly, freezing everyone once again.

Jackson glared at her. "You'd give up your consolation prize to avoid this?"

"In a New York minute."

"It's just a loan, Amy. I'll pay you back."

Amy got up and slipped her dress on, a shudder passing through her. She retrieved her envelope full of cash and handed it over to Mr. Black without a word. She wouldn't splay herself out for these men. She just wanted to go home. Mr. Black pocketed the money and gave her a broad smile.

"That's it, then," Bollinger said. "Are you ready to go, Amy?"

She nodded, feeling very old and very tired. "You're damn right."

Chapter 23

Jake checked the address outside the quiet street near San Francisco's Market Street area. The fog was rolling in and he shivered despite the season. Mark Twain had been right. It was summer everywhere but here, he decided. He went upstairs and knocked on an apartment door on the third floor. The door opened on a chain. "Amy?"

One eye stared back at him. "You have the check?" He nodded and passed it through to her. The door closed. He waited. Nothing happened. He knocked again.

The door opened again. It was still chained. "Amy? Umm, can we talk?"

She eyed him for a long minute. Then the door closed and Jake heard the rattling of the chain. She opened it and let him in. Her face was set in a mask, her eyes blank.

Jake was taken aback. Stupidly, he had expected her to throw herself into his arms. They were finally together, able to pick up where they left off, but Amy hadn't forgiven him.

But then, why should she?

"What's wrong?" he murmured. He took a deep breath, knowing what a stupid question that was.

She exploded. "What's wrong? You can ask what's wrong after the way I was kidnapped, chased like a dog through the woods, exposed to a bunch of leering men—you included—and you have to ask what's wrong?"

Jake stepped back, the blood draining from his face. Deep down, he supposed he should not have been surprised. What happened out there between them was a product of the hunt. Now that she's back home, the horror of the event, and her embarrassment over her liaison with him had turned to anger.

"You waltz in here, thinking maybe you can fuck me again? Is that it? Or maybe you've come to claim your 'prize,' huh?" She pulled her dress off over her head, then unhooked her bra and peeled down her panties. "Okay, Mr. Hunter, here's your prey. Come and claim me!"

Jake let his eyes fall to the ground. He could hear her harsh breathing. "I'm sorry," he said softly. "I can't undo what's been done. We were stupid and cruel."

"You bet your ass you were! I'd like to lock up that arrogant Mr. White or whatever his name is! He's out there now, planning another hunt! And you! You rich guys think you can do anything you want!"

"But-But what about us? Didn't we experience something strange and wonderful?"

Amy made a dismissive sound. "That was—that was—I don't know what that was." She turned away, suddenly embarrassed at being nude. She reached down and snatched up her dress and held it against her. "I'm not sure how I feel about it. I just know that the whole thing was so wrong on so many levels that I can't believe I'm even talking to you."

Jake nodded. "I know. The fantasy seemed exciting, erotic, even. What sounded like some harmless fun for some rich men has ended up hurting someone I've come to really care about."

Amy looked up at him, tears in her eyes. She couldn't speak.

He moved to the door. "I know every time you see my face, it will remind you of your ordeal. I won't bother you again."

Without another word, Jake walked away, closing the door softly behind him.

He left Amy standing there, confused, her anger dissipating like San Francisco fog on a hot day.

Jake morosely trudged down the stairs to his car. His mind reeled with conflicting emotions. If he hadn't pushed for the hunt or if their prey had been another woman, he never would have met Amy. Now that he'd met her, it was all ruined because he'd been an arrogant rich man who thought he deserved whatever money could buy.

He reached the lobby and paused to take a breath before leaving forever.

"Hey!"

He turned, his heart racing. Amy was standing on the landing, her dress loosely tossed over her athletic body.

"I hope you don't think I'm going to let you get out of keeping your end of the deal!"

"Wha? What do you mean?"

"You owe me a dinner out. And I'm choosing the most expensive restaurant in San Francisco!"

Jake's jaw dropped open. Then he smiled.

Chapter 24

"This doesn't mean I'm ready to forgive you," Amy said as she ate her lobster at Fleur de Lys, a very expensive French restaurant she had long coveted, but never could afford before.

"Of course not," Jake said. "You were treated shabbily and no doubt you're feeling abused by the experience. I suggest you demand some serious pampering to make up for it."

She let a smile tug at the corners of her mouth. "Yeah, maybe a bottle of champagne…"

"…a day at a spa…"

"…French perfume…"

"…a pony ride…"

She looked up. " 'A pony ride?' "

They both erupted into laughter.

"Well, I was pretty mad, I admit," she said. "I think I was mad at myself for agreeing to the second hunt. Up until then, I had you guys locked up for the rest of your lives—I mean, if the cops could've tracked you down. But when I signed that contract and agreed to take the money for the next hunt, I became a whore and I didn't like it."

"Please don't say that. To me, you will never be anything less than what you are: An accomplished, professional, beautiful woman who made the best of a bad situation—a situation that I helped cause."

She took another sip of wine. "To tell you the truth, there was another reason I stayed—a reason I don't think I was consciously aware of. Out there, suddenly all of society's rules were turned upside down. I *could* be ravished—unless I got away. That made the whole experience somehow primal. I think that's the reason I reacted the way I did with you."

Jake raised his glass. "Well, you can take your primal emotions out on me anytime."

Amy gave him a small smile over the rim of her glass.

After dinner, which Amy could tell was *very* expensive, Jake gently touched her shoulder as they left the restaurant and waited for the valet to bring around his black BMW. She could feel the heat of his palm.

She reached up and put her hand over his. "Thanks," she said in a throaty voice.

"You're welcome. I enjoyed it."

The valet roared up in the shiny car. Jake tipped him, then held the door for her. When he came around and settled into his seat, she spoke up.

"Tell me the truth about something, okay?"

"Sure, anything." He pulled away from the curb.

"I know you said you had an image of how the hunt would be, and the reality was a lot harder to take. But," she paused, as if trying to find the right words. "Did it turn you on, chasing me down like that?"

"Oh, yes, I have to admit, it did. You were right—there was something primal about it."

"Running around naked might've added to that feeling," she laughed.

Jake slowed the car.

"What? What is it?"

"I was heading to your apartment, to take you home. But I was thinking…"

"Yeah?"

"I have a big ol' place in Marin County. The maid has the day off, so I'm there all alone…"

Amy cocked her head and watched Jake's face in profile. "And?" She wasn't going to make it easy for him.

"Umm. I was wondering if you'd like to play, uh, hide and seek with me?"

Her cheeks dimpled. " 'Hide and seek?' "

"It's a tamer version of the hunt, you see."

"I see. I suppose you'd want to do this naked?"

"Only if you're brave enough, of course."

She smiled that sexy, dimpled smile again and Jake turned the car toward his home. Little was said—both their minds were elsewhere.

Amy was impressed with the house and grounds as he rolled through the electronic fence onto his five-acre estate. He parked out front and escorted Amy inside. They stood, awkwardly for a moment, unsure how to proceed.

"Maybe you could give me a quick tour, so I know where all the good hiding places are."

"Sure," he said. He took her through the house, standing close to her as he showed her various rooms. The smell of her hair, her perfume, intoxicated him. She seemed particularly interested in the master bedroom, upstairs.

"Wow, look at the size of that bed!"

"California King. I like a lot of space."

"You could lose someone in there."

Jake felt if they didn't leave, they might never. "Come on, let's go back downstairs and get started." He walked out awkwardly, his erection pressing against his trousers.

"What are the stakes?" Amy asked when they reached the ground floor again.

"Stakes? Umm. I don't know." He blushed a bit. "I mean, you know what I want if I find you," she murmured.

Amy glanced at his tented pants and remembered their intense fuck during the hunt. Fuck was the right word for it.

"Making love" was far too tame a word for what they did. She felt the heat in her loins return. "So—what? If I win, we still fuck?"

Her bold statement only made Jake harder. "Well, if that's what you want as well, it doesn't seem to matter who wins, does it?"

"No, it doesn't." She began unzipping her dress. Jake quickly followed suit, shrugging off his sport coat and unbuttoning his shirt. "How much of a lead are you going to give me?"

"How much time do you need?"

Amy looked over the house, mentally counting the rooms. "Oh, I think thirty seconds ought to be plenty."

Jake grinned. In seconds, they were both naked. Amy gazed at his erection unabashedly. "I guess that wasn't a banana in your pocket, huh?"

He drank in her lithe naked form: the soft curve of her hips, the pert breasts, the blond hair framing her pretty face. With effort, he turned his back. "I'm counting to thirty now." He couldn't wait another minute to have her. "One, two, three…"

He heard her bare feet padding away down the hall.

When he reached thirty, he turned. Instinctively, he knew where she was hiding. He jogged up the stairs directly to the master bedroom. There, he spotted a small lump under the covers. He jumped on her. "Gotcha!"

She giggled.

Jake slipped in next to her. "This has got to be the worst hiding place ever." Her skin was hot. His hands slipped over her breasts to her stomach. He imagined he could feel her blood rushing through her body, her desire for him finally acceptable. He kissed her hard, pressing his erection against her thigh.

She enveloped him, spreading her legs. "Maybe I'll do better next time."

He cupped his hand over her breast, flicking the rock-hard nipple gently. The tip of his cock touched her wet cunt. "We'll have to raise the stakes," he breathed, kissing her again.

"Shut up and fuck me," she responded and Jake obliged, thrusting his cock deep into her. She gasped and clung tightly to him, shaking with emotion.

They moved together as one. Amy's cunt was hot and wet—it sucked at him. Jake had never felt such heat, such passion from a woman before. There's something to be said about the hunt, he thought, if it results in sex like this.

His strokes drove Amy mad. She heard noises and realized it was her own voice, making inarticulate sounds in her throat. She could see herself outside her body, looking down on Jake's strong back as he thrust harder and harder into her, his buttocks clenching and contracting. Her legs encircled his back. Her mouth was open, eyes staring.

"Oh, god, oh, god, oh, god..." Her orgasm built to a crescendo. Just as she shuddered with an orgasm hitting 8.0 on the Richter scale, Jake came hard within her. She could feel his sperm flooding her womb. Her head exploded—or so it felt. For a moment, she wasn't totally conscious. The room swirled around her.

God, sex with this man was good!

After a few moments, Jake slumped to the side, spent. "If we keep this up," she gasped, "I'm going to get pregnant for sure."

"Yes, you're right." He rolled to the side and leaned on one elbow. "There's just something about fucking you that makes contraceptives inconsequential."

"Something primal, no doubt."

"Yes. But I wouldn't worry about it too much."

She sat up. "What do you mean? We *should* be worried!"

"Nah," he said dismissively. "I figure we're going to want to have three kids anyway..."

She stared at him. "Th-three kids? You and me? Together? We-we don't even really know each other. It's all just sex so far."

"No it's not. And I think you know it. I want you, Amy. I want to share my life with you. Will you marry me?"

"Wow," she breathed out. "You really know how to raise the stakes."

"Well?"

She thought for a moment, then gave him a sly smile. "Let's decide this on the battlefield. One more hunt, a real one — tomorrow. If you win, I'll marry you…"

"And if you win?" he murmured.

She grinned. "We just fuck until I get pregnant and then you *have* to marry me."

Jake laughed and took her into his arms.

About the author:

J.W. McKenna is a former journalist who took up penning erotic romance stories after years of trying to ignore an overly dramatic—and often overheated—imagination. McKenna is married and lives in the Midwest, where polite people would be shocked if they knew what kind of writing was being done in their town.

J.W. welcomes mail from readers. You can write to her c/o Ellora's Cave Publishing at 1337 Commerce Drive, Suite 13, Stow OH 44224.

Also by J.W. McKenna:

Darkest Hour
Lord of Avalon
Naughty Girl
Slave Planet
The Hunted

BESIEGED

Jaid Black

Editor's note: **Besieged is the prequel to Jaid Black's Death Row serial.**

To Arne Hansen:

for your Norwegian translations &
for proving that men like erotic romance too...

this one's for you ;-)

Chapter 1

Nearest Village: Barrow, Alaska

335 miles north of the Arctic Circle near the Chukchi Seacoast

December 1, present day

Her teeth chattering, Peggy Brannigan huddled beneath the warmth of the polar bear skin furs she'd been provided with by her Inupiat Eskimo guide, Benjamin. Wearing a thick woolen coat, three pairs of thermal underwear, two hats, two sets of gloves, and bundled under four polar bear furs, she was still chilled to the bone as the dogsled made its way across the harsh tundra landscape.

"Faster!" Ben instructed the dogs in his native tongue. "Move!"

Peggy's forehead wrinkled as she regarded him. She'd been living and working in Barrow for a little over six weeks now in order to study the ways of the indigenous Eskimos for her anthropological dissertation paper on Inupiaq culture at San Francisco State University. For the majority of the time she'd been in the arctic northern region of Alaska, Peggy's host had been Benjamin's family. She'd gotten to know the teenager pretty well in that time and had found him to be a calm, stoic gentleman not given to outward displays of emotion. That he seemed almost panicked for the dogs to move the sled faster was a trifle alarming to her.

"What's wrong, B-Ben?" she asked, her teeth chattering away from the bitter wind hitting her directly in the face. She kept her tone neutral so as not to appear alarmed. "Have you spotted some wolves on the hunt or something?"

Shit! she thought as she bit down roughly onto her bottom lip. It would be ironic indeed if their dogs were picked off by hungry wolves a stone's throw from the village. Unfortunately, the only way in and out of Barrow was by the occasional chartered airplane or by dogsled, which had given them no choice when seeing to their task but to brave the harsh elements. And the hungry predators.

Making matters that much worse was the fact that it was briskly snowing on the tundra, which caused visibility to be poor. And since the sun doesn't rise near Barrow from November to January, the fact that it was two o'clock in the afternoon did them no good at all. It might as well have been midnight for all of the aid daylight hours gave them at this time of the year.

Peggy took a thorough look around the snowy landscape, trying to ascertain if there were any signs of pack-hunting activity. Her eyes narrowed in question when she failed to spot even a single wolf. The tundra looked so quiet just now that she didn't see any wildlife at all, not even pregnant polar bears nestling into the hibernation dens that the expectant females carved out of snow banks to rest in. She wrapped the furs tightly around her before putting her question to the teenager again. "What is it, Ben? What's going on?"

Ben's almond brown eyes were narrowed into slits, his expression grim. Peggy winced when she saw the riding crop he was wielding lash down onto the buttocks of the lead dog guiding the sled. The dog let out a pained yelp. "We have to get out of here, Peggy," he said as calmly as he could in English, though she could hear the fright in his voice. "You're being hunted," he said a bit shakily.

Peggy's eyes rounded. She swallowed nervously as she again glanced around the snowy tundra.

Ben hadn't said *they* were being hunted, she thought anxiously. He had said *she* was being hunted. There was a big semantic difference between the two and one she wasn't certain what to make of. "What are you saying, Ben?" she muttered, her heartbeat accelerating. The serious teenager never said anything he didn't mean. This was getting weird. And frightening.

"Igliqtuq!" Ben gritted out, the riding crop coming down on the second lead dog. "Move!"

Peggy's heart began thumping wildly in her chest. Her hands knotted into nervous fists from under the polar bear furs. She'd never seen Ben behave this way before. Never. "Ben, please," she said quietly, an acute sense of panic beginning to settle in. "Tell me what's going on."

The rigid lines of his profile said he wasn't inclined to answer her. Not out of meanness or disrespect—not Ben. It was something more, she realized. Perhaps the teenager was trying to protect her from this unknown enemy in whatever way he felt he could. Knowing Ben he probably regretted the fact that he'd alarmed her to whatever presence was near to their position and wished he'd kept his fear to himself so as not to worry her.

It was too late for that. She had gone beyond worry and was nearing the point of panic.

"Please," she breathed out, her aqua gaze wide. "Please talk to me, Ben."

The teenager took a deep breath as he kept at the dogs, enforcing his instruction to move faster with the occasional harsh flick of the riding crop. She didn't think he was going to speak to her, regardless of her pleas, so she was almost surprised when he did.

"Uyabak Nuurvifmiu," Ben said quietly in his native tongue. "Stone dwellers." He swallowed a bit roughly, his dark eyes acutely scanning the surrounding tundra as the dogsled made its way through the bitter wind and harsh snowfall. "I spotted one a few minutes ago."

Peggy stilled. *Stone dwellers. What the hell does that mean?*

The situation just kept getting weirder and weirder. Not to mention more alarming.

"What are you saying?" Peggy murmured. She swiped a spray of snowflakes from her eyes with the back of her wrist. "Ben, I don't understand. What's a stone dweller?"

The endless barren tundra broke, giving way to the beginnings of Barrow village. The occasional ice-coated hut dotted the landscape, ice fisherman scattered about every so often. Benjamin visibly relaxed, a telling sigh of relief escaping his lips. Peggy's gaze never left the teenager's profile.

"Do not worry yourself over it," Benjamin muttered. "There is nothing to concern yourself with now."

Because the threat had passed. For now.

Peggy's eyes narrowed in speculation but she said nothing. If Benjamin wouldn't tell her what was going on then hopefully his sister would.

On a sigh her eyes flicked away from the teenager and toward the village they were fast approaching. An elderly indigenous woman wrapped in wolf furs inclined her head toward Peggy as their dogsled passed by and Peggy absently smiled back.

She hoped she could get Benjamin's sister to talk to her about the stone dwellers—whoever or whatever they were. Perhaps they were only some bizarre species of predator that the Eskimo people revered and therefore would not gossip about, she considered. Or perhaps not.

Whatever the case, she had to know what she was up against before she and Benjamin found it necessary to travel to one of the outlaying villages next week for more supplies.

A chill raced down Peggy's spine, inducing the hair at the nape of her neck to stir. She swallowed a bit roughly when it occurred to her that something—or someone—was watching her.

And that the gaze belonged to an intelligent being.

Chapter 2

That feeling of being watched faded within an hour of arriving in the village and didn't resurface again that day. By the time Peggy nestled into the polar bear furs in the tiny hut and laid down to go to sleep that night, she was certain she'd imagined the entire thing. Her senses had probably been paranoid from the fright Benjamin had given her earlier — a fright that the teenager never did fully explain to her.

It was probably just as well, she decided. The stone dwellers were no doubt some sort of myth, some Eskimo legend as ancient as the people themselves. Nevertheless, Peggy was a scientist through and through and because of that fact, she would make certain she got to the bottom of the story. Not only because that's what a scientist did, but also because she realized that no other anthropologist had ever written of a stone dweller myth. It was possible, she thought excitedly, that she could very well be the first in the field to have ever heard about it.

And that would look impressive indeed in a dissertation paper.

She bit her lip. She would definitely get to the bottom of this. Not just for the dissertation paper, but to satiate her curiosity as well. Peggy had been born with a case of inquisitiveness ten miles long and an ocean wide. She knew herself well enough to realize that she'd never just give up and let this go. Besides the fact if there really was something to be reckoned with out there, she needed to know what that something was for security purposes. She and Ben traveled about too much, were out on the naked tundra far too often, for her *not* to know.

On an exhausted sigh, Peggy turned over within the bed of furs, used her elbow for a pillow, and closed her eyes. First things first, she needed to get some sleep. Tomorrow she would approach Benjamin's sister Sara and hope against hope that the twelve-year-old girl was in a chatty mood.

And that she'd heard of the stone dwellers her brother had spoken of.

* * * * *

"Stone dwellers?" Sara glanced away, turning back to her work outside of the familial hut. It was snowing briskly, so she saw to her task quickly and efficiently. Raising a knife and slashing downward, she beheaded the still-quivering fish with one fell swoop. Her shiny waist-length black hair glimmered from reflections cast off by nearby torches. "No," she said weakly, "I've never heard of them."

Peggy's aqua-green gaze narrowed speculatively. She absently tucked a copper-gold curl behind her ear as she considered what to do next. She didn't want to upset the sweet girl, but she simply couldn't get yesterday's events out of her mind.

Last night Peggy had tossed and turned, unable to sleep. *Hunted.* Benjamin had said she was being hunted. A thought that had plagued her to the point of inducing the first nightmare her unconscious brain had entertained in ages.

Somehow, through the course of the restless night, she had realized that the enigma of the stone dwellers and wanting to unravel who or what they were went far and beyond the desire for glory, or the desire to bedazzle Dr. Kris Torrence—her dissertation advisor—with her discovery. Instead it loomed on the horizon of had-to-know-the-answer-for-self-protection-purposes.

"Sara?" Peggy murmured. "I know you don't want to talk about it. And I know I'm breaking every rule in anthropology by affecting your life rather than merely observing it, but I..." Her voice trailed off on a sigh as she glanced away, her arms coming up to rest under her heavy breasts. "I'm frightened," she whispered.

Sara's body stilled, an action Peggy caught out of her peripheral vision. Peggy's heartbeat soared as she allowed herself to hope for just a moment that the twelve-year-old girl might open up to her. She hadn't lied about her fright. She didn't want to go through even one more sleepless, worried night. She just wanted to verify that the stone dwellers were a myth so she could breathe easy and put it from her mind for the time being. She could find a way to explore the myth later.

"Father says if a girl speaks of them, they might hear, and take her so she speaks of them no more." Sara said the words in a whisper as she set the knife down on the cutting board and slowly turned in her home-stitched leather boots to face Peggy. Her almond eyes, Peggy noted, were wide with anxiety. She lifted the hood of her parka and bundled herself in it. "He says never to speak of them, for the wind has ears."

Peggy's gaze clashed with the girl's. "Do you believe that?" she murmured, her heartbeat picking up again. Her brain told her she was letting herself get freaked out by what amounted to ghost stories told at summer camp, but her body reacted to the child's nervousness as though she spoke nothing but fact. "Do you believe the wind has ears?"

Sara simultaneously sighed and shrugged, looking more like a wizened elder of her people for a moment than a naïve twelve-year-old girl. "I'm not sure. But it's true that my auntie spoke of them once, then disappeared not even two days later." She shivered from under the parka, turning back around to slice and dice quivering fish. "My mother misses the sister of her heart deeply," she whispered. "As do I."

Peggy's eyes gentled in sympathy, though the girl couldn't see that for her back was to her. "I'm sorry, sweetheart. What was her name?"

"Charlene. We called her aunt Chari."

Peggy smiled. "A very pretty name."

"She was a very pretty lady," Sara said bitterly. "Which is probably why they took her." The knife whistled down, severing fish head from fish body in a precise, clean kill.

Peggy's smile faded. She pulled the hood of her parka up, then shoved her mittened hands into the pockets. "Who took her?" She knew what Sara was going to say, but for some perverse reason she wanted to hear the girl say it. Perhaps if she could get her to voice the words aloud then Sara'd tell her a bit more...

Sara sighed, setting down the knife again. She whirled around on her heel to face Peggy, then quickly glanced away. "I'm not trying to be contrary."

"I know," Peggy said quietly. And suddenly she understood that no matter how many times she asked the girl, Sara would never open up. Not about this. "It's okay, sweetheart."

Sara's almond-shaped eyes flew up to meet Peggy's turquoise ones. She nibbled on her lower lip as she quickly glanced around, then cautiously inched her way closer to the anthropologist. "I'll say this and no more," she whispered, gaining Peggy's undivided, wide-eyed attention. "Stay away from the tundra or you'll be as easy to pick off as a fish is to the white bear."

Peggy nodded, but said nothing. Her heart rate went wild again as she fought within herself to remain silent. She prayed that the old adage would ring true and that silence would turn out to be golden, or at least golden enough to keep the girl talking. Psychologically speaking, nobody likes awkward silences, which Peggy was trained enough to know. When faced with awkward silences people had a tendency to prattle, trying to fill up the void. She just hoped Sara would choose to fill this particular void up with the words she needed to hear.

Sara sighed, glancing away again. "They steal women," she murmured. "Women of breeding years."

Thank you Psychology 101.

"But who are *they*?" Peggy breathed out. "Where do they come from—"

"Sara!" Benjamin shouted from the other side of the hut, inducing Peggy to mentally groan. She loved the kid to distraction, but of all the rotten luck...

"Sara, where are you? Father's calling you!"

Sara let out a breath, obviously relieved that she hadn't been caught speaking of things she'd been warned never to discuss. She politely nodded to the anthropologist then turned on her heel, quickly fleeing toward the other side of the hut.

Peggy drew in a deep tug of cold, crisp air and slowly exhaled. Unlike Sara, she was feeling anything but relief. She had gotten some answers, true, but the answers she'd been given only begged for more questions.

And there was something else.

As much as she hated to admit it, as much as she was loathe to even give the idea credence, for the first time since the incident on the tundra yesterday Peggy was beginning to doubt her initial supposition that the stone dwellers were based on myth.

She bit her lip. What if Ben's fears yesterday had been based on cold, hard facts? What if, she thought anxiously, someone really had been hunting her out there?

They steal women. Women of breeding years.

Peggy shivered from under the parka, suddenly not wanting to be outside of the hut alone. Just to be on the safe side, she decided in that moment, she'd make certain she was always accompanied by at least two others from this moment forward until her time in Alaska was done.

She sighed. The situation was getting weirder and weirder.

Chapter 3

One week later

By the time Peggy and Benjamin left the outskirts of Barrow in order to dogsled into a remote village, over a week had passed since their last excursion. More than enough time for the memories of the fright she'd been given out on the tundra to wane in significance, if not die out altogether.

Not one oddity had occurred over the course of the past week. No bizarre feelings of being watched, no worries of being stolen by what had to be mythical men. No nothing.

Peggy had come to believe that Benjamin's family had invented the legend of the stone dwellers as a way to keep Aunt Chari's memory alive. If they believed she'd been kidnapped, when in fact she'd probably been attacked by a hungry wolf or polar bear, then they could believe she was still alive, still able to—hopefully—find a way back to the village one day. Without the legend of the stone dwellers, they had nothing. Just a missing, beloved woman who was no doubt long dead. Sad really.

This hypothesis was the only one that made sense to Peggy for she found it a bit odd that no other anthropologist had ever recorded any Inupiaq legends about the stone dwellers. Nor had she heard any other indigenous person speak of such, with the small exception of Benjamin and Sara.

Peggy smiled up at Benjamin as she took his extended hand and allowed him to help pull her up onto the coach of the sled. "Brrr," she grinned. "Looks like another freezing cold journey."

Benjamin's eyes softened. "You should stay behind. I'm used to this but you—"

Jaid Black

"Need to get used to this too," she interrupted. She smiled warmly, but firmly. "Besides, I enjoy our conversations when we ride over the tundra together." They were trekking back to Chakuru today in order to trade precious whale blubber for homespun parkas. She settled into the cab of the settee-like contraption, nestling into the polar bear furs Benjamin's mother had packed for her. "You never did finish telling me that story about your reindeer herder of a great-grandmother." Her eyes squinted a tad. "What was her name?"

"Sinrock Mary." He grinned, a boyish dimple denting one cheek. "She caused quite a stir in her day. Women didn't own property back then, of course. But granny not only held onto her herd, she did it better than any man."

Peggy chuckled at that. "Sounds like my kind of woman." She smiled fully at Benjamin, causing him to blush and look away. It wasn't until that moment that she realized the teenager had developed a small crush on her, a fact that made her oddly proud. To a sixteen-year-old boy, after all, her twenty-nine years must sound rather old, she mused. "So tell me all about Sinrock Mary."

Over the course of the next five hours Benjamin told her all about his great-grandmother, as well as countless other familial stories. The Inupiaq, she knew, relished a good tale in the same way a chef relishes good food. Indigenous people told their stories with exquisite care, thereby preserving their verbal lore from the taint of time and from the tarnish of contact with outsiders.

They arrived in the small hunter-gatherer village of Chakuru during the sixth hour, none the worse for their ware. The dogs were tired by the time they arrived and Peggy's backside hurt from prolonged sitting, but other than that everything was as it should be.

Peggy smiled at the indigenous children who rushed up to excitedly greet the sled, breathing deeply of the brisk wind while she ruffled the hair of one slight boy. She loved visiting this village for when she looked around it felt like she'd taken a step back in time. And in many ways she had. This village was so remote that it wasn't even on the official Alaskan map.

Benjamin politely inclined his head toward the elder female who'd been speaking to him, then turned to Peggy. "She says her son and his new wife are off visiting family in Nome so she's taken the liberty of fixing up their hut for you." The old woman said something else in a tongue Peggy was not well versed in. Benjamin nodded, then translated. "She hopes you will find the privacy enjoyable and the warmth of the home agreeable."

Peggy smiled, ignoring the nagging voice that told her to keep close to the others and forsake her privacy as she usually did on these trips. Not wanting to offend the old woman, she ignored the voice and nodded. "Thank you," she said, modestly inclining her head. "Your hospitality is very generous."

* * * * *

Wearing a thin white shift Benjamin's mother had stitched together for her, Peggy rolled onto her back from beneath the polar bear furs, a wrinkle marring her brow. From within the throes of deep sleep, she recognized on some surreal plane that something was slowly pulling her out of the world of dreams and into the world of semi-wakefulness. She had that feeling again, that bizarre feeling of being watched...

Peggy's eyes flew open. Her irises immediately tried to adjust to the pitch-black darkness. She could see very little, almost nothing in fact, but she could still make out a shadowy shape on the far side of the hut. She gasped as she sat straight up, her heartbeat accelerating. *Oh my God*, she thought in a panic, *I never should have slept in here alone*.

Her chest heaving up and down from the adrenaline pumping through her system, her heart pounding in her ears, she threw off the polar bear furs and scrambled to her knees. She squinted at the shadowy shape on the far side of the one-room hut, trying to discern what the shape was.

Oh my God. Oh my God! What is it?

Peggy's hands balled into nervous fists as she shot up to her feet. Her breathing was heavy, labored, as if she'd just run a two-mile sprint. Preparing to turn on her heel and dash—anywhere—she gasped when a pale beam of moonlight hit the hut and the shadowy shape turned into…

A parka.

A harmless, lifeless parka sitting on a log chair by the hut's small kitchen table.

Peggy half laughed and half cried. She closed her eyes for a brief moment and exhaled the breath she'd been holding in. Relief—she'd never felt so damn relieved in her entire life. "I'm losing it," she muttered, her fingers threading through her hair and smoothing it back. "I'm a step away from being escorted out of Alaska by the men in white coats."

Taking a deep breath and shaking her head at the mistake, Peggy smiled at her own stupidity. "Get a grip, girl. It was just a…"

Her smile faded as comprehension slowly dawned. A tremor of terror lanced through her as it occurred to Peggy that the parka she'd worn today was hanging near the crude fireplace/stove to dry out. It was not, nor had it ever been, placed on the chair by the kitchen table. She swallowed roughly, her turquoise eyes widening.

Get out of here! Now!

Her heartbeat racing like mad, Peggy prepared to run from the hut when a heavily muscled arm snaked firmly around her belly. She gasped, opening her mouth to scream. A large palm slapped over her mouth before she could get it out, all but muting the wail of fear that erupted from her throat from behind the hand.

Oh my God. Oh my God. Oh my God.

Peggy felt a pinch to her neck a threadbare moment before her body went limp into the awaiting arms of what she assumed was a human predator. The world spinning, her head lulled onto her shoulders and her eyes closed. She fell backwards, passing out.

Her last coherent thought before the blackness overpowered her was that the stone dwellers were real.

And that she'd never live to tell Dr. Kris Torrence about her breakthrough discovery.

Chapter 4

Her brow wrinkled in anxiety, Peggy's eyes slowly flickered open and tried to adjust to the dim light of…wherever she was being held. Her brain had actually awoken a full five minutes ago, but she had yet to open her eyes. She was afraid to look, afraid to find out if she'd been dreaming or if she'd really been—

"Please," the voice of a female softly cried from behind her. "Please let me go home." The voice was frightened, confused. A knot formed in Peggy's throat. "I won't tell anybody," the female vowed, her tone desperate. "I swear I—"

A muffled sound, followed immediately by silence, filled the dimly lit chamber. Peggy closed her eyes tightly, somehow realizing the female had been gagged.

Oh my god. Oh my god. Oh my god.

"Er dama våken?" a man's voice inquired in a language Peggy had never heard before. She stilled her breathing, afraid for him to know she was awake. "Because I'd like to make it back to the village by this evening," he muttered in heavily accented English.

"I'll go check," another man answered, his words spoken in the same Old World accent. "The woman was still knocked out last I looked. But I'll go check the other breeder again now."

Breeder? Peggy's eyes shot open. Her heartbeat accelerated. *Am I the breeder they are discussing?* She quickly closed her eyes, hysterically trying to figure out a way to get away from the men.

"Her breathing is too still," the first man said. His tone was bored. As if he was used to dealing with terrified, captured females all the time. "She's awake. Wants us to think she's asleep—" Perspiration broke out on Peggy's forehead. They knew she was awake. Oh god they knew — "but she's definitely awake."

The second man chuckled. "She wasn't easy to capture, that one. Wolf himself almost seized her out on the tundra last week, but the Barrow boy managed to get her out before his men could surround her.

"Wolf?" the first man murmured. "He hunted her?"

"Ja." *Yes.* "He was very angry when he lost her."

"He wanted her for himself or to sell?"

"I've no notion. It's not my place to question a jarl's son. You know that."

Silence.

"Well then," the first man murmured. "We best keep a good eye on her. Just to be safe."

Peggy swallowed over the lump in her throat. That was definitely not what she'd been wanting to hear.

"Agreed," the second man rumbled out. "If Wolf wants her, we'll be able to barter her for a high sum."

The first man grunted. "We must take her back to our own people first. The men of our village should be able to barter for her first. If none are willing to pay the price we set, then we will barter her to the son of the opposing jarl."

"Agreed."

Peggy gasped when the animal furs that had been draped over her body were unceremoniously ripped off. Her skin chilled immediately, for she was wearing nothing but the thin white shift Benjamin's mother had hand-stitched together for her. She instinctively curled into a ball, both out of fright and to shield her body from the strange men.

"Be still, girl," one of the men muttered as he squatted down beside her.

Her breathing grew labored. Blood pounded in her ears.

The tanned, heavily bearded face of a man in his late forties or early fifties drifted into her line of vision. Viewing him upside down on her back, all she could make out was clear blue eyes, a shaggy mane of black hair, and a full salt and pepper beard. "What do you want from me?" she breathed out.

He shook his head on a grunt, letting her know he'd answer no questions so she needn't ask them. He ignored her after that, causing her distress to grow more acute. "Hurry up and check her over, Rolf," he barked out to a younger blonde man who was squatting down by Peggy's feet. "Make sure she's clean and then let us go."

Wide-eyed, Peggy's already surging heart rate went wild when Rolf placed a tanned hand on either of her thighs and forced her legs apart. *Oh god—somebody help me!* she silently cried out, instinctively rearing up to free her legs in order to kick at him.

She kicked Rolf squarely in the chin, causing him to yelp, then curse under his breath. She tried to roll away, tried to get up and run, but the black-haired man seized her shoulders from behind, locking them against the chilled stone ground in a movement that was as jarring as it was painful.

"Enough!" the older man shouted. "If you do that again, you will be harnessed!"

Harnessed? Oh god! Who are these people?

Thinking quickly, Peggy stilled her body and forcibly calmed herself. The last thing she wanted, she told herself in near hysteria, was to be harnessed. She wasn't precisely certain what that would entail, but it didn't take an Einstein to figure out that it would be harder to escape if the men put a containment device of some sort on her.

The older man grunted, appeased by Peggy's seeming docility. He nodded to the blonde man, telling him without words to proceed.

Peggy anxiously wetted her lips.

"This won't take too long," Rolf muttered in his Old World accent, his hard expression letting her know the kick to the chin hadn't been forgotten. "If you're still and quiet."

She trembled when his rough, callused hands once again parted her thighs. Her breathing grew heavy and sporadic as the thin shift she wore was raised above her head. The shift was then placed over her eyes like a blindfold, making it so she couldn't see who was doing what to her. She bit her lip from worry, embarrassed when the cold air hit her chest and made her nipples plump up.

"Ja," the older man laughed. His hands left her shoulders and trailed down to her breasts. He palmed both of them, kneading them and running his thumbs over the stiff nipples. "Jeg vil feire brystvortene hennes."

The two men exchanged chuckles, which worried Peggy. It was bad enough to endure having her body examined without permission, but when they were speaking of her in another language so she had no idea what they were saying about her…that was downright frightening.

The older man continued playing with her breasts and nipples even as Rolf's fingers began examining her pubic hair. His fingers sifted carefully through the trimmed, coppery triangle, so she rightly assumed she was being checked for lice. He spent a lot of time there, thoroughly examining her soft mons. By the time he finished, Peggy's breathing had hitched, both from fright and from her body's instinctive—and unavoidable—reaction to having her nipples plucked at.

"She's clean," Rolf barked. Peggy let out a breath of relief, assuming that the fondling was over.

"Is she a virgin?" the older man asked.

"Let me look."

Peggy's teeth sank into her lower lip as the tip of Rolf's index finger found her hole. He slid into it slowly, then withdrew. "She's too dry," he said absently. His thumb settled on her clit and applied slow, lazy, circular pressure to it. "I'll let you know in a minute."

Her eyes squeezed tightly shut from behind the blindfold. She could only pray that when Rolf discovered she was most definitely not a virgin that she'd be let go…

A knot of worry and shame formed in Peggy's belly as her body slowly became aroused by the steady fondling. One captor's hands were kneading her breasts and plucking at her nipples, while the other captor's hands were playing with her pussy. His thumb was working its dark magic on her clit, rubbing it and toying with it until her thighs began to softly tremble.

Peggy's head thrashed back and forth on the cold, earthen floor. She gritted her teeth, determined not to come.

"Let it go, girl," the older captor whispered in a thickly aroused voice. He fastened his knees around her head and secured it so she couldn't thrash it around anymore. "Let it go."

Unable to move, unable to protest, Peggy could no more stop herself from orgasming than she could stop night from turning into day. She knew it was inevitable, knew too that she might as well get it over with.

Her breathing grew labored and her nipples stabbed upward, hitting the first captor in the palms. Blood rushed to her lower body, puffing up her cunt for the view of her second captor.

On a growl, Rolf replaced his hand with his mouth. He drew her clit in between his lips and latched onto it, then suckled it vigorously until she was gasping.

"*Oh god.*" Peggy broke on a groan, moaning as her body instinctively convulsed. The first captor continued to knead her breasts and run his thumbs over her stiff, aching nipples, while Rolf sucked on her clit, not stopping until she came a second time, harder and more violent than before.

When she came down from the climactic high, mortification stole over her. What had been done to her was embarrassing enough, but to orgasm for men who had forced it on her was humiliating.

She closed her eyes from behind the makeshift blindfold, feeling more shamed than she'd thought possible. Realistically she knew that her body had merely reacted instinctually, that the orgasm meant nothing beyond a response to a stimulus, yet the feeling of shame lingered nonetheless.

Rolf reinserted his index finger into her pussy hole. This time it slid in easily, her moisture providing the necessary lubrication to probe her. Her nostrils flared from behind the blindfold. She could hardly wait for the asshole to discover that she wasn't a virgin so she would be let go.

"I don't detect a hymen," Rolf said. "She is no virgin."

Peggy's eyes opened from behind the blindfold, blazing with righteous indignation at the bastards.

"Good," the older captor grunted, shocking Peggy. "Virgins don't sell very well on the block."

She swallowed over the lump in her throat, righteous indignation quickly turning into acute fear.

"True," Rolf absently commented as he removed his index finger from her slit. "Virgin bodies don't know how to worship a cock the way experienced pussies do."

Peggy closed her eyes from behind the blindfold, willing herself to breathe. *So much for my theory of being let go*, she thought, as the older captor continued playing with her stiff nipples.

Chapter 5

Peggy's only consolation was that she hadn't been raped—yet. She had no idea what the two men had in store for her, beyond the fact that they planned to sell her "on the block". The situation felt as though it was growing grimmer by the moment. Namely because she hadn't yet figured out a way to escape her captors.

Pulling the polar bear furs she'd been given tightly around her body, Peggy glanced toward the other female captive in the party and noted the terrified quality of the woman's wide-eyed, unblinking gaze. She'd been looking that way the entire trek, she thought, her blue eyes bulging above the gag in her mouth that prohibited screaming. Peggy closed her eyes briefly, fearing that the woman's mind might have snapped.

That was the last thing she wanted for the other captive. If the woman was out of it, it would make it harder for the two of them to communicate so they could escape together. And Peggy was determined that they *would* escape together. Lord only knows whether or not she'd be able to direct the authorities as to where to find this other woman if she managed to escape without her, so it was vital that the other captive went with her.

The two females and their two captors had been riding across the tundra on dogsled for what felt like three days, but realistically had probably been but three hours. The climate seemed to be growing harsher, the snowfall more brisk and chilling.

Peggy shivered from beneath the furs she was swaddled in. *Can I escape with nothing but polar bear furs and secondhand shoes to clothe me?* she warily asked herself. *Does it matter?*

She knew it didn't matter because she would try to escape regardless to how bad the circumstances surrounding any attempt might be. She didn't plan to be around long enough to find out what these two horrid men had in store for her and the other woman. She especially had no desire to hang around long enough to find out what "the block" was. She had her guesses, none of them pretty.

Peggy's gaze flicked toward the two captors at the front of the dogsled. She immediately noted that they were embroiled in a fairly heated discussion in that odd tongue they spoke in. *Now is the time…*

Nibbling on her lower lip, she quickly glanced back toward the other female captive seated beside her, thinking now was as good a time as any to try and establish communication with her. She discreetly reached toward the other woman, then placed a hand gently over hers—

She snatched her hand back, her eyes wide. The other woman's hand was as cold as a block of ice. Peggy's breathing stilled as she narrowed her gaze at the woman's wide blue eyes—eyes, she recalled, that hadn't blinked in hours…

Peggy screamed as she poked the other captive in the chest. The woman's icy body slumped over, the sound of one of her frozen vertebrae snapping as easily as a chicken bone chilling Peggy to the bone. "Oh my god!" she hysterically wailed, feeling as though she might vomit. "She's dead! Oh my god—she's dead!"

A stinging backhand across her face instantly quieted Peggy. She whimpered, her hand instinctively flying up to the cheek that had been slapped brutally enough to bust teeth. She was lucky, she thought as tears welled up in her eyes and the metallic taste of blood filled her mouth, that she had only garnered a cut to the inside of her mouth and that her teeth hadn't been busted by the impact.

"Shut up, woman!" Rolf spat in his Old World accent. "Or you will be gagged!" He glanced toward the dead captive, his expression irritated. "Throw her off the sled if you can't stand the sight of her, otherwise wait until we stop and I'll remove her. But do not," he seethed through clenched teeth, "cry out like that again."

Peggy's eyes widened at his callous disregard for human life. A woman had died—died!—and he was no more concerned about it than she imagined he would have been had one of the dogs of the sled team died. Actually, she thought bitterly, he'd probably be more upset if it had been one of the dogs instead of this nameless, faceless woman who was nothing but lost chattel to him.

Her nostrils flared as she locked eyes with the disgusting excuse for a man. She had never hated anyone or anything more than she hated this man in this moment. She said nothing, just showed him her hatred through her narrowed, aqua gaze.

When he broke her stare, she turned her head to the right and spat out a gob of blood that had accrued in her mouth. She watched the mingled blood and saliva land in the snow, staining the pristine white a crimson red. She idly wondered how much more of her blood would be spilled before she was free again.

"Don't try anything stupid," Rolf murmured without looking back at her. "The last one who tried something stupid was your friend there."

Peggy's eyes widened. She thought back to an incident that had occurred before the party of four had taken off by dogsled. The other woman, hysterical, had tried to run. It had been Rolf who had tracked her down, Rolf who had found her, Rolf who had put her on the sled so that she was already docilely sitting there before Peggy had been brought out...

He had *known* the other captive was dead, she thought, her breathing stilled. Oh god—he was the one who had made her that way!

Her hand flew up to cover her mouth. Rolf, probably not wanting to leave a trail behind, had loaded the woman's dead body onto the sled so he could dispose of her later, when they were further out onto the desolate tundra.

Nausea churned in Peggy's stomach, threatening to expel itself. She closed her eyes and took a deep breath, forcing herself to calm down in the process. The last thing she wanted to do was vomit. She knew it would gain her nothing but another slap, or worse.

Help me, God! she mentally screamed. *Please help me!*

"What the...?"

Peggy's head shot up at the sound of Rolf's perplexed voice. Her eyes narrowed at the back of his head as she tried to discern what the matter was.

"Damn it!" the other captor bellowed. "Damn Valkraads!"

"How many?" Rolf calmly asked, his hands reaching toward and picking up a crossbow.

"One, two maybe."

"Then we can take them."

Their speech reverted to the foreign tongue after that, ensuring that Peggy was kept in the dark. She had no idea what a Valkraad was, nor could she see any other people or animals in the immediate vicinity to clue her in as to what was going on.

Peggy teeth sank into her bottom lip, her heartbeat accelerating. It occurred to her that now, while the two men were distracted, might be her only chance at escape...

A deafening war cry startled her, causing her to gasp. The snowbanks seemed to come alive then as four men camouflaged by polar bear skins seemingly exploded from out of the tundra itself. Her eyes widened as she watched the armed men stampede toward the dogsled on foot, preparing to cut it off at the pass by any means necessary.

Oh god, Peggy thought, her eyes wide and breathing labored. Who were these men? Her salvation or the bringers of an even worse fate?

A tall, heavily muscled male threw off his polar bear fur as he gave his war cry, simultaneously revealing that he wore nothing beneath it save tight buckskin trousers that looked almost Native American in origin and a pair of tough leather boots. His tanned, muscular chest was completely bare, his sunny blonde hair flying against the wind as his icy blue eyes narrowed at her captors.

Peggy froze, her mind in complete shock. How could the man's body withstand such frigid temperatures? How could — *forget it, Peggy, just run! Run! Run! Run!*

Her muscles corded, her body in fight-or-flight mode, Peggy jumped from the ongoing dogsled and landed on her face, simultaneously knocking the wind from her gut.

Fight it, Peggy! Get up and run!

Under ordinary circumstances she doubted she would have been able to rebound so quickly, but then these circumstances were hardly ordinary. She shot up to her feet, gasping for air even as she took off, fleeing under the dark skies of the cold tundra.

She ignored her banged up knee, ignored the cheek that had been slapped so hard it felt like it was on fire, ignored the icy snow that coated her face from when she'd fallen. She instead concentrated all of her energy on running while scanning the snowbanks for a den or a burrow she could hide in.

She heard shouting behind her, heard too the whizzing sound the arrows made before they found purchase in the flesh of men — which men she hadn't a clue. She ignored it all as she ran faster and faster, panting for air, desperate to escape.

Peggy's eyes widened when she heard footfalls gaining on her. *Oh no!* she thought in bubbling hysteria. *Oh God, please let me get away!*

But the sound grew alarmingly closer — the sound of packed snow crunching under the weight of leather boots...

She braved a quick glance over her shoulder. She cried out when she saw that it was *that* man chasing her down — the grim looking blonde with the wolf-blue eyes, the heavily muscled body, and the hellish war cry.

The grim looking blonde man who was even taller and broader up close than he'd been at a distance.

Her eyes wide and breathing labored, Peggy whipped her coppery-gold head back around and ran faster still, discarding the polar bear furs as she made a mad dash across the tundra, not wanting the skins to weigh her down. She wore nothing but the white shift and secondhand leather shoes now, yet her body was perspiring as though she was overheated instead of freezing.

Run! she mentally screamed. *Run! Run! Run! Run!*

She cried out when his big body collided with hers from behind, then screamed as she began to topple forward to the ground, knowing as she did that if he fell on top of her he'd probably break a few of her ribs. His hand shot out at the last possible second, his arm simultaneously snaking around her belly, preventing both of them from falling.

"Please!" Peggy cried out desperately, her arms and legs flailing as he plucked her off of the ground. "Please let me go!"

The man said nothing, merely held her body out and away from his body, her back to his front, while she kicked and screamed. Pretty soon she had an audience, for three of his men were in the process of surrounding her, all of them chuckling as they watched her arms and legs flail about like a panicked fish. "Let me go!" she screamed, anger quickly replacing terror. "Damn you, let me go!"

And still he said nothing. He continued to stand there, stoic and resolved. He held her away from his body until she'd kicked and screamed to the point of fatigue, only then lowering her to the ground and setting her on her feet.

Mentally drained and physically exhausted, her coppery-gold curls plastered to her head with perspiration, Peggy offered the giant no resistance as he bodily turned her around and gently wrapped animal furs all over her body. She couldn't bring herself to make eye contact, didn't have the wherewithal to so much as glance up at him.

His large callused fingers ran through her soaked hair, stroking it away from her forehead before he tucked it up into a furred hat that came down far enough to cover her ears. One of his hands roamed down her head and over her face, stopped at the bruise she'd garnered on her cheek from being slapped by Rolf, and rested there.

Confused, Peggy glanced up. Her brow wrinkled, not sure what to make of the unnamable emotion she saw emanating from those icy blue eyes in an otherwise stoic face. Was he sorry that Rolf had hit her? Or, she thought wide-eyed, did he feel that was something only he himself should be allowed to do to her?

She swallowed a bit roughly when his harsh gaze found hers, realizing at once that this man would be a formidable enemy. As his rough, callused hand gently probed her cheek, she had no remaining doubts as to what had become of her former captors.

Now, she thought warily, her eyes wide as her teeth sank into her lower lip, she had to wonder what would become of her at the hands of this new, and far more dangerous, captor.

Chapter 6

Geirwolf Valkraad loaded his captive onto the dogsled, the adrenaline of first the attack and then Peggy Brannigan's capture, still coursing through his blood. He felt dangerously out of control still, a state of mind and body he'd been entertaining ever since his brother Aevar had spotted the woman in the hands of the Hallfreor clan's resident vultures.

The Hallfreors, Geirwolf knew, condoned selling females to men desperate for breeders, as though the women meant no more than, and were just as barterable as, whale blubber. The Valkraad clan was the only one out of four settlements in total that practiced the old ways and did not approve of this method for obtaining wives. The general feeling being that there was no honor in buying a wife, only in displaying the cunning and bravery inherent in stealing one.

Outsiders, he realized, would disapprove of their ways. Not that he particularly cared. This was how he had been raised, how his father had been raised, how his father's father had been raised, and so on.

The custom of stealing breedable women was as old as their people, and one Geirwolf couldn't fathom ever coming to an end. When his ancestors had sailed to this side of the globe around 950 A.D. in their longboats, they had brought their values with them. Where those values had long since been lost in Old Norway, they had stayed the same, untainted by time, in New Norway. A fact their people were proud of.

Geirwolf took the seat behind Peggy on the dogsled, nestling her between his muscled thighs to keep her warm. He could feel her trembling, knew that she was scared of him. He gently rested a palm on her shoulder, letting her know by his actions that he meant her no harm. He called out to Aevar then, telling him to get the dogs moving.

Peggy Brannigan, he thought, his cock stiffening against her back. He had been hunting her for weeks. His body had been aching from the need of her for weeks. It seemed too good to be true that she was sitting at his feet even now. She was his for the taking, her voluptuous body soon his to plunge into at whim.

The dogsled took off, leaving Geirwolf free to consider the woman sitting before him. In his culture, he knew, she would be considered a rare beauty. Hair the color of autumn at sunset, eyes like the ocean, and her body…

His people coveted full, hippy, belly-dancer physiques in women, finding the fleshy look as erotic and earthly sensual as his ancestors once had. Perhaps it made females appear more fertile and capable of birthing strong babies—whatever the reason her figure was perfect to him.

His hands trailed down her sides, then into and under the polar bear furs. She gasped, startled, when his palms cupped her breasts, his thumbs running over the swollen nipples. They were so firm and ripe—he wanted to turn her around and suck on them here and now.

"Brother," Aevar called out in their tongue, breaking him from his thoughts. "I spotted some wild animals up on the right. We best keep an eye out for them."

"I'm watching." Geirwolf released Peggy's breasts, an action that seemed to calm her. He took no offense, for he realized it was her preference that he didn't touch her at all.

But, he thought as he gave her full breasts one more gentle squeeze, that was only her preference for now.

Chapter 7

Peggy chewed on her lower lip as she glanced to the right, absently taking note of the dogsled racing neck-to-neck with the one she was seated in. Two men were riding in that one, while Peggy, her captor, and a fourth man she took to be named Aevar were all riding over the tundra in another one.

All of the men, Peggy noted, had that same lost-in-time look about them that her original captors had possessed. They were tall men — veritable giants in terms of their extreme height and brawn. She accurately guessed that all of them were somewhere in the range of six and a half feet or better, weighing in at two hundred and fifty to three hundred pounds of solid muscle mass.

Stranger still was the way they were dressed. They reminded her of Vikings from old with their long manes of hair, their intricate arm bangles, and their buckskin clothing and leather boots.

Even the tattoos they sported appeared like ritualistic markings rather than mere decoration. The man who had captured her, for instance, the one whose legs she was currently sitting between, was heavily tattooed on both his back and his left arm. His back, she had noticed before he'd wrapped himself into an animal skin, was completely covered with intricate and mysterious markings, the bluish-green pigment expertly woven into his skin. His bulging left arm carried the design of a dragon, the long serpentine body snaking up from the wrist, the head making its appearance at the bicep.

It was as if all of these men had been catapulted from the year 850 in Norway and then thrust into modern day Alaska, never realizing along the way that the heyday of their people had long since passed. She wondered how such a noticeably different culture of men could have gone on so long without being found out by what they would deem to be outlanders. From an anthropological standpoint, Peggy was fascinated. From a personal standpoint, she was terrified.

Peggy's body stiffened as her captor's large, callused hands reached under the polar bear furs she was swaddled in and palmed her breasts from behind. He had done this once before during the trip, but she had thought he was going to leave her alone when he'd abruptly ended the contact in order to speak with Aevar in that odd tongue they spoke in.

This captor, Peggy thought warily, was nobody's fool. He wasn't even giving her a chance at thinking she might escape him, for rather than sitting at the front of the sled with his comrade, he had chosen to sit at the back with Peggy kneeling before him, her back to his front.

"I want you to send word to their people," her captor said in heavily accented English to Aevar, the man guiding the dogsled. His hands gently kneaded her breasts, "that they need to collect their dead." He paused. "And I want them to know why," he said in a soft but commanding tone.

She assumed he was conversing in English only because he'd wanted her to understand what he was saying, assumed too that he had been speaking about her original captors, the ones they'd killed out on the tundra. She swallowed roughly, the memory a portent reminder of what could happen to her if she tried to escape.

"It's done, Wolf," the other man said. "I'll take care of it as soon as we return to the village."

Peggy's eyes widened slightly. *Wolf…*

The man the original captors had spoken of? The man who had been hunting her out on the tundra that day Benjamin had gotten scared?

Shit.

Her breathing stilled when her new captor's thumbs rubbed over her distended nipples. She breathed in raggedly, fright and arousal at war in her body. He seemed to sense her tumultuous reactions for his forefingers got into the action then, his thumbs and index fingers plucking at her stiff nipples with expert precision, massaging them again and again from root to tip.

Peggy blinked a few times in rapid succession, determined to shake the arousal off. She expelled a shaky breath, uncertain as to what she should do.

But, of course, there was nothing to be done. She had no choice in the matter, and her captor didn't seem inclined to stop fondling her anytime soon.

He played with her breasts throughout the remainder of the trip, a journey that was beginning to feel endless. She could feel his steel-hard erection poking against her back, could hear the arousal in his thickly murmured words as he bent his head to her ear. "All will be well, Peggy Brannigan—" She stilled, surprised that he knew her name—"I vow that no harm will come to you by my people's hands." She swallowed, but nodded, grateful for at least that much revelation of what was to become of her.

He didn't speak to her again after that, but his hands continued kneading her breasts and massaging her stiff nipples. After several minutes of this attention, she found it harder and harder to fight the arousal, and eventually gave up altogether.

Breathing deeply, Peggy's heavy eyelids closed as she leaned her coppery-gold head back on his knees. Her captor seemed pleased by that, for his mouth lowered to her neck and placed tantalizing kisses at her pulse while his hands continued to toy with her breasts.

Peggy sighed softly. With her erogenous zones being manipulated as they were, she began having small orgasms that couldn't be stopped. By the time the dogsleds came to a halt that night and her captor removed his hands from her breasts, he had given her four small orgasms. A fact that she could tell pleased him immensely.

This intimate play went on for the next three days and nights. When they would camp for the night, her captor Geirwolf—Wolf to his comrades—would sleep beside her in the makeshift tent, fondling her body into orgasm, but never making a move to penetrate her or to force her to touch him. She knew he was hard the entire time, and yet not once did he lose control. He brought her to peak more times than she could count, his hands always roaming about and caressing her nude body.

From both an anthropological and personal standpoint, Peggy knew that the man's methods were getting to her. Psychologically speaking, it was difficult at best to fear a man who brought you endless pleasure and asked for nothing for himself in return. At worst, it was impossible...even if that man was holding you captive against your will.

During the days when they were riding by dogsled, her captor would stroke and fondle her breasts the entire time, giving her mini-orgasms. Sometimes he would even stroke her pussy, though he never permitted her to have big climaxes this way.

This method of conditioning served to work her up, making her body so aroused that by the time nighttime came and they were alone in the tent together once again, she was less and less resistant to his touch. He would fondle her in earnest then, not stopping until she came violently at least twice, whereupon she would fall asleep in his arms, feeling safe and unnervingly secure.

By the third night, Peggy found herself willingly spreading her legs for Geirwolf, so he could play in her cunt. His icy blue eyes raked over her naked body, over her puffed up pussy, watching intently as she used her fingers to spread her labial lips for him.

It was unnerving—knowing that she was being conditioned as easily, if not more easily, than Pavlov's Dog.

"Very beautiful," he murmured, his hot, sweet breath close to her cunt. It was one of the few things he had ever said to her, for he almost never spoke. "Would you like me to kiss you down here?"

Peggy wetted her lips. "Yes." He'd never done that to her before. Until this night he had used only his hands. Her breasts heaved as she expelled a shaky breath, her nipples jutting upward. "Yes, please kiss me down there," she whispered.

Her captor lowered his face between her legs, wasting no time as his mouth latched around her clit and vigorously suckled it. She groaned, arching her hips, grinding her cunt into his face. "Yes," she whispered, her head rolling back and her eyes closing. "That feels so good."

He sucked on her clit harder, growling low in his throat. It was the first time she'd ever heard him express an out-of-control emotion and she found that it only fueled her own fire. She shouldn't want this, her mind rebelled. And yet her back arched as a breathy moan rushed from her lips, her legs simultaneously wrapping around his neck as if to draw his face in closer and closer to her aroused flesh.

Peggy gasped as her orgasm approached. Her breathing grew labored and her hips flared up. She was going to come hard, she knew. She was going to—

"Wolf!" a man's voice called out from the other side of the tent. Peggy sighed, feeling an odd sense of disappointment when her captor kissed her clit, then raised his face from between her legs.

"Ja?" He drew up to his knees and opened the tent flap for the other man to poke his head through.

Peggy recoiled, her eyes wide when Aevar's head emerged into the tent. Aevar, a grim looking but handsome dark-haired man, had been quite kind to her these past few days, but she was embarrassed at the thought of yet another male seeing her naked. Already three had—her original captors and Geirwolf.

She tried to close her thighs so Aevar couldn't see her nudity, but her captor wouldn't let her. Geirwolf's large hand fell to her still-aroused cunt, playing in it as if marking his territory. She blushed when Aevar's gaze fell to her exposed pussy.

Neither male paid her any more attention as they conversed with each other in their preferred tongue. Geirwolf continued to stroke her pussy in a possessive, branding fashion, but otherwise had his attention focused on what was being said to him.

She felt calmed once again when it became apparent that her body was not the focal point of attention. She climaxed with Aevar's face still poking through the tent, unable to stop her body's reaction. Geirwolf ceased playing with her clit after that, his fingers absently stroking through her soft pubic hair instead as if petting her for a job well done.

A few minutes later, rather than resuming the sexual play after Aevar left as she'd assumed he would, her captor fell tiredly onto his back, his callused hands running through his sunny blonde hair on a sigh that coming from any other man would have sounded weary. Since his eyes were closed, she allowed herself to study him for the first time since she'd been captured.

He was a handsome man, she had to admit. Very harsh looking with his never-smiling expression, chiseled features, and icy blue eyes, yet handsome nonetheless. His body was pure muscle—the hardest and biggest musculature she'd ever seen on a male up close and personal. And he was tall, very tall. Probably closer to seven feet than six. She was certain that if he stretched out completely, his legs would poke through the tent flap.

Peggy's gaze fell to his exposed, and highly erect, manhood. Geirwolf always slept naked, the same as he made her sleep, but he never did anything about it. She found herself wondering why. She supposed he just wanted her to get accustomed to his nudity, accustomed too to how big his swollen penis was, before he upped the proverbial ante.

She glanced away. Her gaze trailed back up to his grim, exhausted face. He looked weary and troubled, yet she knew he'd never tell her why.

She supposed she shouldn't care why.

Peggy bit her lip, briefly contemplating the insane thought of lowering her mouth to his stiff cock and latching her lips around it. To comfort him? To give him pleasure? She hadn't a clue.

Sighing at her troubled thoughts and equally disturbing compulsions, she flipped over onto her side, her back to him, and released a ragged breath. This was ridiculous. What she had contemplated doing to him was downright obscene given the circumstances.

Peggy's nostrils flared, anger coursing through her. She would not succumb to that man ever again, she vowed. If he meant to rape her, then he would have to do just that. Never again would she willingly spread her thighs for him. Never again would she allow him to fondle her without a fight. This was her life, damn it! She wasn't going to give it up, wasn't going to forget who she was, just because it seemed more expedient at the moment.

Stay focused, Peggy. Stay focused...

"You belong to me now."

Peggy's breathing stilled at the sound of those softly spoken, matter-of-fact words. She bit her lip, comprehending the fact that he'd never let her go easily. For whatever reason—breeding, sex, whatever—this man wanted her. And he meant to keep her.

Geirwolf rolled onto his side, his muscular, dragon-tattooed arm draping over her body. She swallowed roughly when his fingers found the soft coppery curls between her thighs and began to idly sift through them.

"I hope you accept this soon," he murmured in that Old World accent. He placed a kiss on her shoulder. "I would not have you unhappy."

Peggy said nothing, though she felt like crying. How would she ever escape him? she wondered. How could she ever hope to elude a man who never left her side?

There was a long silence and then, "If you would not have me unhappy," she whispered to him, "you would free me."

His fingers stilled in her pussy hair. "I will make you happier than you thought possible, Peggy Brannigan." The words would have sounded arrogant coming from anyone else, but from him they sounded like a mere statement of fact. His fingers resumed their lazy exploration of her intimate curls. "This is a promise."

Peggy bit her lip. She thought back on the customs of the ancient Vikings, particularly about their method for acquiring brides. Panic bubbled up inside, constricting her throat.

Way back when if a Viking marauder coveted a woman he simply stole her away, keeping her as a captive until she'd fallen in love with him and no longer desired to leave him. Only then, when he was certain of her devotion, was she allowed to roam about unattended, her freedom semi-restored.

Peggy took a deep breath and expelled it. She prayed to God the custom had been lost in antiquity to the stone-dwellers.

* * * * *

Who were these people that had taken her captive? Peggy wondered for what felt to be the millionth time as Geirwolf helped her from the dogsled. Their journey, she had been told, was over now, yet she couldn't make out the beginnings of a village anywhere within viewing distance.

She took a thorough look around, noting that the climate had grown harsher, snowier, than the climate she'd been stolen from. What was going to happen to her now? she asked herself. Had she been brought here as a breeder, as Sara had indicated, or as something else entirely?

"Let's move," Geirwolf barked to his men. "I want us out of sight as quickly as possible."

Peggy's eyebrows rose. She offered her captor no resistance when he took her by the arm and guided her toward what appeared to be an empty snowbank, but wasn't. Her brow furrowed as she watched the heavily muscled Aevar grit his teeth, his muscles bulging, while he manipulated a snowbank that was no snowbank. Instead it was a well-concealed, ice-coated stone door leading to only who knows where. The door eventually gave, and Aevar quit gritting his teeth.

She was intrigued despite herself. Peggy estimated that they were deep into the belly of the Arctic by now — perhaps still in Alaska, perhaps not. Wherever they were, it was in a climate so harsh, so remote and seemingly uninhabitable, that nobody ever bothered to venture here let alone build villages in so rough an atmosphere.

She swallowed over the lump in her throat. Apparently the stone-dwellers lived in villages that went below the ground or were carved out of caves. She couldn't imagine what else the stone door could possibly lead to.

Peggy took a deep breath, realizing at once that nobody would ever think to look for her here.

She chewed on her bottom lip. They wouldn't even know that here existed.

Chapter 8

Gawking at her surroundings, Peggy couldn't seem to close her gaping jaw as they walked through the ice-coated stone door and into another world, a world that looked as though it had been frozen in time a thousand and some odd years ago, never to be touched by the hands of progress. Or what outsiders would consider to be progress at any rate.

The narrow passage they had been walking through abruptly widened, and an entire civilization previously unknown to her was revealed. Throughout the mammoth underground cave, which was lit by lanterns, smaller caverns had been dug out of the walls. To the left were a series of small merchant dens where citizens were even now bartering for goods, and to the right there were about six grocer dens, all of them specializing in the selling of different foods.

All of these fascinating bartering dens were sealed off from the corridor she was walking through by doors, the doors actually being no more than black iron bars that were lifted up and out of the way during hours of commerce.

Peggy's brow furrowed as an odd awareness went through her. Something, she thought anxiously, was troubling about this scene. Something she couldn't quite pinpoint. She was tired, she realized, so maybe it would take a while before she figured it—

She gulped. Her eyes widened.

Oh. My. God.

Peggy's jaw about unglued when it dawned on her that every woman in the vicinity—every woman!—was either totally naked or, at minimum, topless. *No way!* she thought angrily. *No way am I walking around like this!*

"Is this," she hissed, her nostrils flaring, "some kind of a sick joke?"

Aevar chuckled, immediately recognizing the source of Peggy's distress.

She came to an abrupt halt and spun around. She took a moment to glare Aevar into silence, then turned her narrowed gaze to her captor. "I'm not kidding!" she said in a venomous whisper. "I refuse to walk around like that!"

Geirwolf frowned. "It's the accepted dress for females amongst our people."

"What dress? They are naked!" Peggy's eyes widened in horror as she quickly glanced around, her anxiety-ridden gaze drinking in the sight of so many nude women. She turned back to Geirwolf, her aqua eyes pleading. "I feel like I'm going to be sick. I can't do this. I absolutely cannot walk around like that."

His eyes softened a bit. "All will be well."

"All will be well?" Her nostrils flared to wicked proportions. "All will *not* be well!" she spat. "I am a scientist, not a...a...stripper!"

His gaze hardened, telling her without words that, insofar as he was concerned, the subject was not up for negotiation. "You will learn to accept this."

"Why did you take me?" she breathed out, her voice desperate. Her breathing grew labored as acute panic settled in. Her hand balled into a fist. "Why don't you let me go?"

"Peggy..."

But she had no interest in whatever it was her captor had been about to say. "Go away!" she screeched, batting at the hand that was trying to rest on her shoulder in a gesture of reassurance. "Go away!"

In an instinctive action born of fear and self-preservation, Peggy dashed around Geirwolf before he could catch her and ran toward the stone door leading back to the outside. Her heart felt as though it was going to beat out of her chest as her arms and legs pumped like mad, trying to outrun him.

"Help me!" she screamed, not for the benefit of those inside who she knew would offer no assistance, but in the futile hope that somebody on the outside world would hear her. It was a small chance at best, but the only real one she had. "Please help me! I was stolen by a crazy man!" she wailed as she ran toward the door. "Please somebody help me!"

Peggy ran smack into a male she didn't recognize, knocking the wind out of her as she tumbled backward to the ground. She gasped for air, panic enveloping her again when Geirwolf and Aevar plucked her off of the ground.

The other two men who had rode with them out on the tundra were there too, men whose names she didn't know—men whose names she had no desire to know. They spoke to Geirwolf in their common tongue, so she had no idea what they were saying to him.

Peggy screamed as loudly as she could, her arms and legs flailing madly as the men picked her up and carried her away. "Please somebody help me!" she cried, tears welling up in her eyes. "Oh god—please!"

It took all four of them to restrain her, a testament to the adrenaline coursing through her blood. She'd never felt so panicked and out of control as she felt at this moment.

For the first time since this surreal situation had begun, it dawned on Peggy that these men would never let her go alive...

Unless outsiders came in and forced them to release her.

* * * * *

Geirwolf ran a hand over his stubbly jaw, then wearily plopped down onto the tavern bench. He thanked Hilda, the tavern master's wife, when she set a mug of hot tea and whiskey before him. He threw a silencing look at his brother Aevar, who was still busy chuckling over Peggy's screaming and kicking episode.

"'Twas amusing," Aevar sniffed, his tone defensive.

Geirwolf frowned. "Mayhap to you, but not to me. She called me a crazy man. Did you hear her speak thusly of me?"

The two brothers continued their conversation in Old Norwegian, the untainted version of it that was centuries old and more familiar to them than English. Old Norwegian was a tongue so different from modern Norwegian that nobody in the motherland would even recognize it in the present day.

The English spoken by their people, on the other hand, was of the modern variety, taught to them by captured American brides. Hence, when males of the Valkraad clan spoke in English, it tended to be through a romanticized, feminine view of the world. A fact their mother often had a laugh about.

Aevar snorted. "She is distraught. She will come to accept you in time. You know this, Wolf."

Geirwolf said nothing to that, merely frowned at his hot tea and whiskey. "I just hope the trainers aren't too tough on her. I don't want her spirit broken, only amenable."

"The trainers know what they are about, brother. Many of them are married women who have been dealing with captive brides for years."

"True."

Aevar grinned. "Hurry up and breed her and then she can leave the breeding stalls. Mayhap you won't worry about her fragile—" He coughed into his hand, knowing it was a ridiculous word to describe Peggy given today's outburst— "spirit. If she's always near to you, that is."

Geirwolf gave him a semi-smile. "I'll let her settle in." His expression grew thoughtful, serious. "But," he murmured, "I'll begin as soon as the ceremonial words are spoken."

Chapter 9

Peggy was certain she had died and gone to hell. Gone were her clothes, gone were her shoes, gone was her dignity, gone was her life, period. In its place was Hell with a capital H.

Upon awakening from the effects of the sleeping agent she'd been given last night to help calm her, the first thing Peggy noticed was that she had been bathed without her knowledge or consent and was now completely naked. Even her pubic hair had been trimmed into a tiny triangle, the coppery arrow pointing down to her hooded clit. The rest of her mons was as smooth as baby skin.

The second thing she noticed was that her feet were painted with intricate designs in a henna-based pigment. She had no idea why this had been done to her and harbored a strong suspicion that she wouldn't like the answer.

The third thing Peggy noticed upon waking was that she was being corralled in an area with a bunch of other naked women, some of them English-speaking and weeping in the way she felt like doing, some of them giddy and speaking that odd tongue she couldn't place. All of them had henna designs etched into their feet. Again, the anthropologist in her screamed, this didn't bode well.

Especially since in some cultures, such as India, painted feet often preceded marriage ceremonies. *Shit.*

"Good morn, everyone."

Peggy's head shot up at the sound of the feminine voice. Her gaze immediately honed in on the speaker, noting her to be in her late thirties or early forties. The woman was naked like the rest of the females in the corral, her pubic hair trimmed down into a tiny blonde triangle. Also like the other females, her feet were painted. The only noticeable difference insofar as Peggy could see was that the speaker was wearing gold arm bangles around either bicep, whereas the other captives hadn't been adorned with them.

"My name is Ivara," the speaker continued in that same accent as Geirwolf's, "and I, along with the help of two other Valkraad women, will be helping...err...how do you say?...*prepare* you for your new lives."

Peggy frowned. This definitely did not bode well.

"Please stand up." The speaker smiled warmly. "I would like for everyone to introduce themselves."

Peggy blinked. She had been kidnapped, drugged, and otherwise humiliated, yet she was supposed to stand up and introduce herself as if nothing was amiss? Yeah. Right.

"I said stand up." Ivara's smile dissolved, replaced with a harsher expression when none of the English-speaking females took to their feet. Peggy snorted at that, wondering what kind of reception this woman had possibly expected from them.

Ivara narrowed her eyes at the English-speaking women, Peggy included. "I repeat," she said softly, motioning toward a male guard without breaking eye contact, "stand *up*." The guard, a huge, thickly muscled male close to seven feet in height, raised his hand, revealing the bullwhip he held. He lashed it once on the ground for effect, the severe sound shocking.

Peggy's eyes widened. She scurried to her feet.

Shit.

"Very good." Ivara smiled warmly again, her earlier irritation seemingly forgotten. "Now, you will introduce yourselves to me and to your other trainers. When we have finished, I will then tell you more about what will be expected of you in New Norway."

New Norway, Peggy thought as she nibbled on her lower lip. So she had been right—this society was some offshoot of the ancient Viking lineage. If she'd been studying this culture as an anthropologist, she would have been fascinated. As a captive, however, all she felt was unadulterated fear.

Peggy listened with half an ear as the captives introduced themselves one by one. When it was her turn to speak, she muttered out a half-hearted "my name is Peggy," then spoke no more. Apparently she'd said enough, for the whip-wielding giant didn't make any moves to hit her.

Before long Ivara was speaking again. "Every female in this area has been claimed as a Valkraad bride." Her smile was proud. "Of this, you should feel fortunate—"

"Fortunate!" an English-speaking captive spat out, interrupting the trainer. A beautiful caramel-colored woman of what looked to be mixed Afro-European lineage, her light brown eyes were as frantic as her speech. "Well, I don't! And I want to go home!"

Ivara's eyes narrowed at the recalcitrant captive. The whip-wielding giant took a step forward, but Ivara held up a palm and shook her head. She muttered something in her tongue to the giant, who apparently grumbled his agreement. "Michelle, is it?"

But Michelle didn't answer. She was too busy crying. Peggy reached out and took the young woman's hand, noting that she couldn't be more than nineteen. "It'll be okay," she whispered. "Just stand by me and relax. We'll figure something out."

Ivara's eyebrows rose. Peggy could tell the trainer was wondering what she had said to Michelle to calm her. Michelle was now standing close to Peggy, quiet and semi-collected, though still sniffling.

"Well," Ivara said to Peggy, her gaze a bit suspicious. "I see you are a quick study." She shared a look Peggy didn't know the meaning of with the whip-wielder behind her, then turned back to the crying captive. "Michelle," she said softly, "I realize this is difficult for you. At least right now. But things will look up."

Michelle said nothing. She huddled her nude body closer to Peggy's and continued sniffling. Peggy put her arm around her, offering silent comfort.

"It's best," Ivara continued, "for you to accept your fate and adjust to the new life waiting here for you in New Norway." Her gaze remained fixed on Michelle, though Peggy realized the trainer was speaking to all of the female captives.

Ivara was silent for a moment, but finally smiled warmly to the captives and continued her speech. "I had thought to begin by telling you of what your future mates will expect in their wives, yet I see now that topic must wait." She sighed, and oddly enough, Peggy was fairly certain the action was genuine. Whatever it was Ivara was about to tell them, it appeared that she held no desire to do so. Peggy gulped.

"A happy fate awaits every woman here in the breeding stalls," Ivara began. She stopped when the English-speaking captives, Peggy included, gasped at her words.

"Breeding stalls?" Michelle murmured to Peggy, her gaze unblinking. "Oh my god."

Peggy swallowed against the lump in her throat. Her thoughts exactly.

"Unless," Ivara said firmly, "you refuse to accept your fate." She whispered something to the giant behind her, then turned back to the captives. "I want everyone to form a single file line. We will begin this morn's instruction by visiting first the Commons and then the Dungeon of Shame." She turned around, then cocked her head to look at the captives from over her shoulder. "I think it's best," she said softly, "if you see what becomes of recalcitrant brides."

Peggy and Michelle glanced at each other warily, then broke apart to form a single file line. Peggy stepped in front of the younger woman, unconsciously trying to shield her from the trainers and the whip-holding man whose name they had still not learned.

The other captives got in line behind them, all of them looking solemn. Even the women native to New Norway seemed to tense up at the mention of this field trip.

Peggy stepped in line behind Ivara and another trainer, preparing to follow them to wherever it was the captives were to be led. The giant with the whip and the third trainer took their places at the end of the line, keeping a vigil to make certain nobody dared try to escape. The giant's eyes flicked over Peggy's body as he took to the end of the line, a gesture that made her conscious of her nudity. She blushed, her hands instinctively flying up and cupping her breasts to shield them.

He grunted and continued on. She blew out a breath of relief.

As the naked women were led from the large underground earthen room they'd been closeted in, Peggy noticed that there were several stone doors dotted all around it, leading to what were presumably connecting chambers. She was curious as to what all the doors led to, at first assuming that they permitted natives to reach the "breeding stalls" from various points in the primitive underground kingdom. But she assumed incorrectly, a fact she was quick to find out.

Peggy's heartbeat accelerated when the captives passed by an open door. She immediately recognized the rooms for what they were—trysting chambers. A place for the men of New Norway to be with their captives in private. A place where they could—she gulped—breed them.

The individual rooms were much smaller than the large inner chamber they were adjoined to. There was enough space in each one to fit two people and a bed, but nothing else.

Her thoughts turned to young Sara. She wished she had heeded the twelve-year-old Inupiat girl's whispered advice more than words could say. She had been a fool to dismiss the stone-dweller legends as just that. Her present circumstance was living proof of the fact that the tales were true.

What now, Peggy? How the hell are you ever going to break out of this place?

Escape was looking grimmer by the moment, she silently conceded. Even if she could find a way to sneak from the breeding stalls, she had no idea where they were located in conjunction to the ice-coated stone door leading to the outside. And even if she made it to the outside, what then?

On the way here their party had driven by dogsled for days without seeing a single soul. How in the world would she ever manage to find civilization on foot?

Peggy shivered as the captives were led from the breeding stalls and down a frigid earthen corridor that wasn't heated. Her nipples immediately plumped up, the ice-cold air making them stiff. Her hands dropped to her sides, her nipples too sensitive to continue palming her breasts in a fruitless mission to keep them covered. It wasn't like it mattered anyway, she thought resignedly. Anybody passing by could see the rest of her naked body.

"Here is our first destination," Ivara announced in thickly accented English. She stopped before a tall door made of wood and iron bars, then turned around and faced the group, her expression grim. She threw a blonde curl over her shoulder. "In this room," she said in an authoritative tone, "you will bear witness to what becomes of recalcitrant brides. This large cavern we are about to enter is called the Commons Chamber, or more simply, the Commons." She waved a hand towards the door. "The females inside have been sentenced as laborers here. They see to the needs of *all* males covetous of their bodies, rather than just the *one* male who was to be their husband," she said pointedly.

Peggy could feel Michelle tense up from behind her. She held out her hand without turning around, letting the young girl clutch onto her for comfort. Lord only knows, Peggy thought as she nibbled on her lower lip, that she could use a little comforting herself.

The captives were ushered in single file through the door and paraded in front of a group of loud, boisterous — and huge — men. The men immediately took notice of the captives and began to whistle and shout out things at them in their native tongue.

Peggy tensed up, yelping when a heavily muscled blonde man ran his callused palm over her exposed breasts, squeezing them as she walked past. Ivara said something to him in a reprimanding tone, to which the giant only grinned.

Peggy blew out a breath of relief even as her heart rate picked up. She quickly forgot about the man who'd groped her, concentrating instead on gawking at her surroundings.

Males were seated all around the Commons, a room that looked to be a large tavern. Naked women were scurrying about everywhere, waiting on tables and catering to the men here. The only difference Peggy could see about the females in general was that rather than having a small triangle of hair between their thighs, all of their pubic hair had been shaved bald. Also, their feet were not painted. Otherwise, they looked the same as everyone else here. Naked, she thought grimly.

But that wasn't what was making her gape at the people inside of the tavern. The upsetting part was that Ivara hadn't lied. The bodies of these poor women were being groped and fondled, pinched and played with, and none of the males seemed to be asking for permission. Men were pulling the serving maids down onto their erect laps and doing whatever they wanted to do to them. Suck on their nipples, shove the women's faces down to give them blowjobs, fuck them—they did everything.

Peggy's hand unconsciously flew up to cover her mouth. She watched in morbid fascination as the body of a beautiful brunette was stretched out onto a table by four men. The men were laughing and boisterous as they sucked on her stiff nipples and played in her cunt. They spoke in their native tongue so she had no idea what was being said.

"Oh my god," Michelle whimpered, threading her fingers through Peggy's. "Look what they're doing to her."

Peggy could only nod, her gaze snagged by the scene across the room. She watched as the woman was turned over and placed on all fours. A groaning Viking sank into her pussy from behind, his fingers digging into the flesh of her hips as he rode her body hard. The woman gasped, giving another male the opportunity to shove his swollen cock into her mouth.

The men rode her body hard, stuffing her cunt and mouth full of cock. She could hear the woman moan from around the penis fucking her face, and didn't know what to make of it. Were they moans of pleasure? Or, she thought wide-eyed, moans of horror at what was being done to her?

When a third man slid underneath the serving maid and began to frenziedly suck on her nipples, Peggy looked away. She glanced toward Michelle, feeling sickened by how ill the girl looked. "Are you okay, honey?" she whispered.

"No." Michelle closed her eyes briefly and took in a deep tug of air. When she looked at Peggy again, there were tears in her eyes. "I'm a virgin," she quietly admitted.

Peggy's breathing stilled. *Good lord in heaven*, she thought, *please don't let these men violate a child.* "How old are you, sweetheart?"

"Eighteen. Almost nineteen," she whispered.

Peggy nodded. She squeezed Michelle's hand. "What do you want to do?"

"Escape!" the girl fervently whispered. "I can't believe this has happened. I feel like I'm living a nightmare!"

Peggy couldn't disagree with that. But, she thought warily, if they tried to escape and were caught, she'd never forgive herself if Michelle's first time with a man was the result of a gang rape in the Commons. "What if we're caught, sweetheart? You don't want to end up here," she said quietly. She glanced around, noting that Ivara was watching them like a hawk. "The trainer hasn't taken her eyes off of us," she murmured.

"I know," Michelle softly cried. She closed her eyes tightly and took another deep breath. When she opened them again, she seemed a bit more in control but not by much. Peggy could only imagine how frightened she must be—she was eleven years older than the girl and even she couldn't recall ever having been more scared than this.

"I think we should go through with the marriages," Peggy whispered. "And escape when everyone isn't watching us so closely."

"Look at this beauty!" a drunk Viking interrupted in heavily accented English as he pulled Peggy down onto his lap. Her gaze wildly darted toward Ivara, looking for an escape from this groping. But Ivara was embroiled in a conversation with her whip-wielding giant.

Oh shit, she hysterically thought. *Of all the times to not be watching me like a hawk...*

Peggy's heartbeat sped up and her breathing grew labored as the muscular man set her on his knee and began kneading her breasts. His blue eyes so much like Geirwolf's were narrowed in desire, his words thick. "Such a pretty little girl you are," he said hoarsely, his thumbs grazing her nipples, causing her to gasp. He rotated his hips a bit, letting her feel his solid erection under her bottom. "Do you feel the treat I have waiting for you?"

If she had met him on the street, she idly considered, she would have found the man dangerously handsome with his piercing blue eyes and dark hair. But under the conditions in which she found herself in, naked in the lap of a man who'd had too much to drink, all she felt was acute fear. "Please don't," she breathed out, her breasts heaving from her labored breaths. "I—I—I'm promised to another!" she stuttered out in a rush.

His hands stilled on her breasts, though he didn't release them. She bit her lip as she watched his gaze stray down to her cunt. She realized by the disgruntled look on his face that having pubic hair apparently meant that you were protected from all this, a fact that made her release a pent up breath.

The man muttered something in his Viking tongue, his irritation as he released her obvious. Peggy scurried to her feet, preparing to dash away, when he pulled her in close, her nipples just inches from his awaiting mouth.

"Tonight, I have no luck," he mumbled. The man's blue eyes, glazed over with inebriation and lust, fixated on her nipples as he flicked them back and forth with his forefingers. He played with them for a solid minute like a cat with two toys, making Peggy bite her lip.

Peggy's body reacted to the stimulus, arousing her, a fact that didn't sit well with her. But between standing naked in front of a clothed man and watching helplessly as he fondled an extremely sensitive erogenous zone, there wasn't much she could have done to prevent it.

But eventually, thank the lord, he stopped. She'd never felt so relieved as she felt the moment he put her away from him, apparently having decided he'd contented himself enough after rubbing her nipples for a while.

She turned to Michelle, who looked pale as a sheet. There was nothing she could say to comfort her and they both knew it.

Peggy took a deep breath. It was either succumb to the training or end up here. She would definitely not end up here. Nor would Michelle. A situation like this would break the young girl's mind.

"Well now that you have all had a taste of the Commons," Ivara called out, "it's time to see what happens to the females who are given no more chances after receiving their punishment." Her eyebrows rose. "The next stop is the Dungeon of Shame."

Peggy and Michelle glanced at each other. They both implicitly understood what the other was thinking without saying it aloud:

They found the Commons deplorable enough. By the time they left the Dungeon of Shame, they both knew that Ivara would have won and they would succumb to whatever fate lay ahead.

* * * * *

"I'm going to faint," Peggy said weakly, muttering to herself. "I'm going to fucking faint."

Her eyes wide, nausea churning in her belly, Peggy stared surrealistically at the caged women, the jails they had been locked into dangling a few feet above the ground. The women inside of the cages had been blindfolded and chained down on all fours, depriving them of movement and visual stimuli.

The caged women were all naked, of course, their legs obscenely tied apart so that the bald, awaiting flesh between their thighs was exposed to any man who entered the dungeon. Viking men walked by and fondled the display of cunts in any manner of their choosing. If a man took a fancy to one, he asked the warden for the skeleton key to the cage, opened the iron door, grabbed the female prisoner by the flesh of her hips, and sank into her pussy from behind. If the woman came during the sex session, then the male would throw food bits into her cage when he was finished fucking her, treating her like an animal at a petting zoo.

Peggy's hand flew up to cover her mouth, horror lancing through her. She leaned against an equally terrified Michelle, feeling as though she might faint. *This is not happening*, she thought. *For all of his faults, I can't believe Geirwolf would condone a society that would do this to women.*

By the time Ivara called an end to the twisted field trip, Peggy was resolved to see the marriage to her captor through. She wouldn't try to run, or help Michelle escape, until she was fairly certain they could make it without being recaptured.

Because one thing was for certain: there was no way in hell either she or Michelle would end up dangling from the ceiling in suspended cages, their bodies splayed out for any man to take.

Peggy closed her eyes briefly and took a steadying breath, her body shaking slightly from nerves and ice-cold fear. There was no way in hell.

Chapter 10

On the eve he was to trade vows with Peggy, Geirwolf prowled towards the *thing* — the meeting place of the leaders of New Norway — with another of the groomsman. Anticipation of wedding and then breeding his future wife making his cock stiffen and his stomach muscles clench. The ceremony, he hoped, would be the easy part. It was the ritualistic bedding to take place after the binding ceremony that had him worried. He hoped Peggy would prove agreeable to it...or at least tolerant of it.

Geirwolf had no idea how much resistance she would give him when first he tried to mount her, though he had often heard it said that Ivara was an accomplished trainer capable of breaking down a woman's reticence in mere hours. He took comfort in the knowledge that already three days of training had gone by, and more importantly, already Peggy had agreed to speak the ritualistic words that would bind them together for all time.

He had no idea of the methods Ivara had used to train the captive brides, yet found himself hoping that the rumors were true and Peggy would prove amenable to not only his troth but also his lust. After all, the sooner he impregnated her, the sooner she could be moved from the stalls and into his own cavern.

"Which of the females is yours, Wolf?" his cousin Ragnar asked, breaking Geirwolf from his thoughts.

Ragnar, only twenty-three years old, had set aside his bachelorhood in lieu of marriage the moment he'd clapped eyes on the eighteen-year-old Michelle, an exotic beauty he was to wed with this eve. It had taken Ragnar a solid month of planning, but the young and handsome blonde Viking who had been named for the mutual grandfather their ancestry shared from over a thousand years ago, had managed to snag his captive bride on the third attempt. Not bad for a warrior of twenty-three.

"Peggy," Geirwolf absently replied, his thoughts focused on the night ahead. He and his cousin turned left when the earthen corridor narrowed and followed the dimly lit path to the Hall of Ceremony, the officious meeting place of the *thing*. Geirwolf's father, the jarl, would be performing the binding ceremony for himself and Peggy, as well as for four other couples, Ragnar and Michelle included.

"Ah! She's quite a beauty!" Ragnar grinned. "But then so is my Michelle." He sighed, sounding every bit a young man in the throes of his first true passion.

A semi-smile tugged at the corners of Geirwolf's lips. He knew precisely how his cousin felt.

* * * * *

Wide-eyed, Peggy gulped as she watched Geirwolf stride into the large, cool cavern with a younger man at his side. Her intelligent gaze raked over the giant she was to marry this evening, noting at once how finely he was dressed.

He wore a long tunic made of black silk with tight, form-fitting black braies underneath it. His tanned, not to mention massively muscled arms were bulging from around the gold arm bracelets he wore at either bicep, the dragon tattoo on his left arm ending just above the bangle.

She glanced down at his hands and felt desire flicker in her belly. She blinked, shaking the feeling off, realizing as she did that he had conditioned her body to respond to them during the long dogsled ride to New Norway. Apparently, she thought grimly, he had conditioned her so well that her body responded to the mere sight of his masculine, callused hands.

Well, she sniffed, her chin going up defensively, she could hardly be blamed for her reaction.

Geirwolf smiled at Peggy, throwing her completely off guard. She hadn't been expecting that. The man was not big on smiling. The small gesture made his grim features appear less threatening, laugh lines making his already handsome face that much more appealing.

Oh damn, she thought as she nibbled on her lower lip, *he's already getting to me. Some martyr you make, Peggy! Stop it. Stop it. Stop---*

Geirwolf's icy blue eyes flicked over her naked body, then narrowed in desire. Peggy squeezed her thighs together, her body's embarrassing reaction to his intense perusal causing her to momentarily forget how much she hated him, how much she loathed the man for making her his captive bride. She glanced away, clearing her throat and blinking.

"There he is," Michelle whispered from beside her. "Oh Peggy, I'm so scared!"

Peggy's gaze followed Michelle's line of vision directly toward...*Geirwolf*? Her heartbeat accelerated as the adrenaline kicked in. *Oh damn*, she thought. *Are we both to be his brides?* Her nostrils flared. *Bastard!* She decided to ignore the fact that jealousy was knotting in her belly.

As Geirwolf drew closer, she realized that Michelle had been speaking of the young man at his side—a very nervous, and she had to admit quite handsome, young man who was staring at Michelle like a lovesick puppy.

Peggy let out a breath of relief, then hesitated, wondering why she'd cared to begin with. Wouldn't a bride who wants nothing at all to do with the groom actually prefer a polygamous marriage? After all, she conceded, it meant that he'd be less likely to bother her for sex all the time.

Her eyes drifted up to the six-pack belly rippling beneath his tunic. Yeah, she frowned, sex would be a real bother.

"Remember the cage," Peggy absently said to Michelle. "This won't seem so bad if you think about that horrible cage."

Michelle's body stilled. "Right," she whispered. "How could I forget that."

Geirwolf came to a halt in front of Peggy, his possessive gaze raking over her breasts and then her trimmed coppery-colored mons. She instinctively sucked in a breath, unwittingly causing her breasts to heave.

"Hello Peggy," Geirwolf murmured. "I've been waiting for this night for weeks."

Which meant he'd been watching her long before she'd been abducted. Her eyes widened.

Long, callused finger threaded through her own. She glanced down to where their hands were joined and took a deep breath.

"You have nothing to fear from me," Geirwolf said softly, but firmly. "I will treasure you and your body always. Before long, you will come to me of your own doing, eagerly seeking out my arms."

Peggy blew out a breath as he guided her toward the center of the cavern. That, she thought resignedly, was precisely what she was afraid of.

Chapter 11

The well-lit cavern was grandly decorated for the ceremony taking place, gold and bejeweled dragon statues peeking out of the earthen walls, a large tapestry of Viking longboats hanging over the double doors. Natives began to pour in by droves, packing in to watch four of their warriors take four women as wives in a tradition as old as their people.

Peggy would have been fascinated by the pomp and circumstance had it not been directly affecting her life. And, she thought through seething teeth, had she not been forced down to her knees, naked, and made to sit deferentially at Geirwolf's feet as if paying homage to him.

Naked and on her knees aside, Peggy hesitantly admitted, she was still fascinated by it all. She felt as though she'd stepped through a portal and been transported into another time and place—Norway in the ninth century instead of the Arctic Circle in the twenty-first. Even this business of sitting submissively on her knees before the bridegroom she knew to be a distinctly medieval tradition. Such had been a common gesture peculiar to certain regions of Europe in marriage ceremonies back then, though the modern romanticization of ancient days gone by never told you that much.

She could feel the gaze of the men in the cavern looking her over, checking out her nude body. The realization that she was being assessed and evaluated, not to mention ogled, made goosebumps break out on her skin and her nipples harden.

Peggy blew out a calming breath, then looked back up to Geirwolf who was listening intently to whatever ritualistic words were being said in that foreign tongue they shared. She didn't move a muscle throughout the entire ceremony, just stared meekly at Geirwolf as though there was nobody else in the entire cavern except for him…just as she'd been instructed beforehand by Ivara to do.

When she was prodded to say yes, she blew out a breath and answered yes. Ten minutes later when the gregarious officiator said some words that caused the natives inside the cavern to cheer, she rightly assumed she had well and truly been wed.

Peggy nibbled on her lower lip. Good lord, she was married to the man who had kidnapped her.

* * * * *

Geirwolf watched Peggy's eyes widen in alarm when two of his father's men plucked her off of the ground from where she'd been kneeling at his feet and tied her down, naked and spread eagle, onto one of the three ornate beds that had been brought into the *thing*. Michelle, because she was a virgin and her husband would have bloodstained sheets to show the assembled crowd, was squirreled away into the breeding stalls to be breeched by Ragnar in private.

Because Peggy was no virgin, she was forced to endure being publicly mounted that no warrior might make a future claim stating that her marriage to Geirwolf had not been truly consummated. If a warrior could make such a claim, it made Peggy fair game. And Peggy, he thought tensely, was definitely not in the game.

He disrobed before the ornate consummation bed, his gaze never straying from Peggy's. He could tell she was embarrassed at being splayed out like this in front of so many, so the faster he covered her the better.

He could not blame her. Until this very moment, he had not given much thought to how callous it was for the men to gather around and watch a new, and presumably terrified, bride be mounted. His wolf-blue gaze narrowed at his younger brother Bjorn whom he noted was staring a bit too intently at his wife's exposed cunt. Bjorn merely chuckled as a reply, his eyes so like Geirwolf's twinkling at his anger.

Geirwolf's jaw clenched. He had heard that an inebriated Bjorn had pulled Peggy down onto his lap when she'd been taken to the Commons by Ivara and the other trainers. That had been insulting enough, but this—

"Relax, Wolf," Bjorn teased in their native tongue. "I am but looking at the wench."

Geirwolf said nothing, though he continued to stare challengingly at his brother. He knew it was ridiculous to behave so jealously, yet he couldn't seem to help himself. Always, the ladies had found Bjorn pleasing to be with. He was handsome with his black hair and wolf-blue eyes and his personality wasn't so stark as Geirwolf's. Bjorn didn't carry the responsibility of knowing he would be leader to their people one day so he could afford to be less rigid in his thoughts and conduct.

The brothers stared each other down until, inevitably, Bjorn's smile broke. He nodded respectfully at Geirwolf, the unspoken promise to respect Peggy there in his gaze.

Geirwolf grunted, appeased. He continued disrobing, throwing his finery to the wayside and stepping before his bride fully nude and fully aroused. He saw her nibble on her lower lip a bit as he grabbed his thick cock by the root and walked toward the consummation bed. Her stare grew wider as he came to stand before her and he found himself wondering not for the first time what it was she was thinking.

Geirwolf took a deep, steadying breath as he crawled onto the bed and settled himself between Peggy's splayed legs. He had been waiting to plunge inside of his wife for what felt like years. He had spent the better part of every day these past few weeks fantasizing about what her warm cunt would feel like wrapped around his erect cock.

He didn't want to rut on top of her like an animal, yet he deeply suspected that was precisely what he was about to do. For weeks he had hunted her. For days he had endured the knowledge that she was in New Norway, yet inaccessible to him...

His gaze flicked down to his manhood then back up to a nervous Peggy. His cock was so erect that the engorged ruby head was painful, his balls so tight he knew this first time wouldn't last long.

Geirwolf's gaze clashed with Peggy's. Now, he thought possessively, his muscles clenching, she was all his.

* * * * *

Peggy's teeth sank down into her lower lip as she watched Geirwolf settle himself between her legs. Cheers and jests were filling the cavern as males clamored closer and closer to watch the new husband fuck the new bride. Thankfully the cheers and jests were being spoken in their native tongue rather than in English, so she didn't have to suffer from embarrassment at knowing what was being said about her.

Still, she had her ideas. All of them mortifiying.

Peggy could feel how intensely her nude body was being stared at by the men in attendance. And perversely, or perhaps inevitably, her body reacted to the knowledge. Her nipples were so stiff that it was painful, her cunt wet. When all she could do was lay there, splayed out and tied down, there wasn't much reaction she could give other than the seemingly innate ones her body was eliciting.

Being stared at through hooded eyes by so many handsome men was more arousing than it should have been. Being coveted by so many handsome men while confident in Ivara's promises that no man but Geirwolf was permitted to touch her was more arousing than she wanted it to be. And then there was Geirwolf himself...

He had conditioned her body well, she thought nervously. The moment he had started disrobing, that steel-hard, muscular body of his visible, she had become wet. By the time his long, thick cock sprang free from his braies and pointed eagerly upward against his navel, her breathing had become increasingly labored, as if she was panting.

He grabbed his penis by the base, the swollen organ looking even more impossibly virile juxtaposed against the backdrop of his heavily muscled arm with the menacing tattoo of a dragon snaking up it. Her breasts heaved once, the nipples aching.

Geirwolf settled himself atop her and Peggy realized that, bizarre or not, she wanted him inside of her. For the past three days she had been mentally trained for this moment by Ivara, and for the three days prior to that she had been bodily conditioned by Geirwolf himself to respond to him.

He placed the thick head of his penis at her wet opening, then gazed down at her, his icy blue eyes narrowed in desire. The large, callused palm of his left hand cupped her right breast and gently kneaded it even as he settled his big body between her thighs.

The fact that he had decided to arouse her using her right breast, the breast not visible to the onlookers crammed against the bed on her left, further warmed her to the man. She rightly suspected he was trying to keep her aroused so the impending sex wasn't at all painful, while simultaneously shielding the intimate act from intruding eyes.

She blinked, finding such an act from Geirwolf incongruously sweet with the hard, relentless image of him she'd formed in her mind. And he was right—touching her was much more intimate than the actual process of fucking her. Any animal could fuck. It took meaningful caresses and touches to make the act something more, something infinitely deeper.

"All will be well, Peggy," Geirwolf murmured, his voice husky with arousal. "We need to do this but once in front of the others. After that, our lovemaking will always be private."

Lovemaking—he thought of what they were doing as lovemaking. She blinked twice more and glanced down at his chest.

Peggy blew out a breath and glanced back up at him—at her husband. "I know," she whispered. She smiled a bit, making his eyes widen. Apparently he hadn't expected such a conciliatory gesture so soon. And, truthfully, she was surprised she had made one too. Nevertheless, his thoughtfulness in this regard deserved at least that. "But thank you for reassuring me."

Geirwolf seemed to want her more after that. His gaze was burningly aroused, his muscles clenched so hotly she could see perspiration breaking out on them. He shifted his weight onto his right elbow and, away from the view of onlookers, removed his left hand from her breast and used it to help insert the head of his swollen cock into her pussy.

Peggy moistened her lips, desire knotting in her belly. Her breasts heaved dramatically, inducing Geirwolf to release his cock once the head was securely inside of her and play with her nipple—again so nobody else could see.

But Peggy was beyond the point of caring who saw. She arched her hips as best as she could and threw them at him, blatantly inviting him to come all the way inside.

Geirwolf groaned a bit, sounding half-delirious. His jaw was tense, his jugular vein bulging. Without any further preliminaries he gritted his teeth and, on a louder groan, impaled his cock into her flesh, seating himself to the hilt.

Peggy gasped, an uncontrollable moan escaping from her throat. Thoughtfully, which she was beginning to learn was the norm where he was concerned, Geirwolf lowered his face so his sunny-blonde hair cascaded down the left side of her own face, shielding the reactions she made against the cheering crowd like a fan.

"Thank you," she whispered, her voice clearly aroused. He groaned a bit more in response, apparently loving the sound of her voice mingled with words of gratitude he hadn't expected to hear from her for a long time. But, again, his thoughtfulness in this regard deserved the words.

He took her hard then, thrusting in and out of her pussy like an animal, mounting her as though he meant to brand her insides. Peggy gasped, her head falling back against the bed, partially unshielding it to the others. She closed her eyes and enjoyed the sensation of being stuffed full of Geirwolf's cock, way beyond the point of caring what anyone saw or thought.

"Fitta di er så deilig," Geirwolf said thickly, his teeth gritting. He pumped her hard, thrusting in and out of her suctioning pussy faster and faster. "Your cunt feels so good…"

She came instantaneously, the arousing words coupled with the arousing fuck her undoing. She could imagine what they looked like to the others, could imagine the way his steely buttocks looked as they clenched and contracted while his cock rooted inside of her. She managed to suppress the sound of her muffled moan by biting down on the sinewy strength of her husband's shoulder instead and groaning into it.

Geirwolf growled, then fucked her harder. The sound of flesh slapping against flesh filled the cavern, competing with the sound of jests and cheers. He buried himself inside of her over and over, again and again, making her come until her pussy was sopping wet.

After she came again, Peggy could feel Geirwolf's body tensing up above her own and she knew that he was getting ready to orgasm. She opened her eyes and glanced up at his harsh face, wanting to see that second of vulnerability that would engulf his features when he came.

"I'm going to fuck your pussy all day and night," he gritted out, his voice hoarse. "Forever."

Geirwolf fucked her impossibly harder, greedily impaling her flesh over and over again. He thrust into her ruthlessly, reveling in the pre-climatic nirvana that was somehow always better than the climax itself.

He held himself over the edge for as long as he could, mercilessly riding her cunt. His rough palm kneaded her bare breast, branding it, while his cock possessively branded her pussy.

She could hear the heady sound of their flesh meeting, the sound of her cunt trying to suck him back in on every upstroke. He pounded into her flesh once, twice, three times more. And then, unable to hold himself back any longer, he thrust into her cunt as deeply as he could go, closed his eyes tightly, and came on a loud groan.

Peggy studied his face, mesmerized by that few seconds of vulnerability that she knew would be there when he had an orgasm. As his body convulsed atop hers, as his teeth gritted and his muscles tensed, she watched his expression keenly, fascinated by the way his grim features lightened for that threadbare moment in time and he appeared no more menacing than a butterfly.

"You're all mine now, Peggy," Geirwolf said between pants as he collapsed on top of her. His breathing was labored, his voice hoarse and firm. "Forever mine."

She bit her lip and looked away, nervously wondering how long it would take before her reticence had been completely chipped away.

Chapter 12

Swaddled in polar bear furs, Peggy sucked in the cool air of the above-ground courtyard, basking in the feel of fresh air and snowflakes hitting her squarely in the face. She knew Geirwolf wasn't supposed to bring her here yet, at least not until she was an impregnated, fully-fledged member of their people. And yet he'd snuck her out into the courtyard anyway without Ivara knowing—yet another token of affection from him.

"This is what we call a zaba root," Geirwolf murmured as he plucked a vine-like plant from the ground. He snapped it into halves and showed her the sap that leaked from it. "It's used by our women to make sweets with. Taste it." He smiled as he handed the root to her. "It's much like sugar."

Peggy slowly held out her hand, then tentatively reached for the plant. Her aqua gaze clashed with Geirwolf's as their fingers brushed against the other's. She bit her lip and glanced away, then nervously raised the root to her lips and sucked the sweet sap from it.

His eyes tracked the suckling movement her lips made. She blushed, wondering if he was imagining his cock in place of the plant.

It had been a little over a week since she'd been married and already the man was getting to her in a big way. His persistence at wooing her was practically extraordinary, for she had been far from agreeable from the get-go. Peggy didn't want her husband to befriend her, nor did she want to love him, so she'd behaved as petulantly as possible toward him and his overtures of kindness ever since their wedding night.

Clearly, her grand plan wasn't working.

Geirwolf had met each of her acts of defiance—which ranged from simply ignoring him to screaming when he tried to touch her—with patience and understanding. He had stayed all but glued to her side the entire past week regardless to how she behaved, allowing her to vent her frustration and anger without becoming angry in turn.

Clearly, his grand plan was working far better than hers.

Peggy wasn't the type to easily form close emotional connections with other people, and especially not with men. She didn't trust males much and never had with the singular exception of her—may the lord rest his soul—father.

It had been Peggy's experience in relationships that when the going gets tough, men get going. She had expected that Geirwolf would be no different, so she had been more than a little surprised when she'd come to realize that no matter what she did and no matter how badly she behaved, he would never give her up. She didn't know whether to be further frustrated or downright flattered by this realization. Her mind said the former, but her heart said the latter.

"Why are you doing this?" Peggy whispered. Her head came up as she lowered the root from her mouth. "Why?"

His eyes crinkled uncomprehendingly at the corners. "I'm not sure I follow—"

"—Why are you keeping me?" she interrupted. She sighed and glanced away. "No matter what I do you still want to keep me. So let's lay our cards on the proverbial table, okay?" She took a deep breath and met his gaze. If she didn't leave this man soon she'd never want to leave him, she thought in a panic. "What will it take to get you to let me go?"

He stared at her for a long moment, but said nothing. He blinked, then glanced away, his gaze staring absently at the moon overhead. "There is nothing you can do, nothing you can say, no defiant act you can make, that will get me to release you," he said softly.

"But why?" she asked pleadingly. "Make me understand. Make me understand why you can't let me leave and take a native woman as a wife—a woman who can better deal with being taken from everything and everyone she's ever known."

Geirwolf sighed. "Peggy…"

"Yes?"

He looked at her again, his grim features uncharacteristically vulnerable. "Would you believe me if I said I was sorry for what's happened?"

"I don't know," she said honestly.

She was surprised by how much it hurt to hear Geirwolf admit that he felt as though he'd made a mistake when he captured her. But then she could hardly blame him. She'd been far from kind or accepting of him since the very beginning. But then she could hardly blame herself. Because she hadn't wanted to be captured in the first place. Her emotions, it seemed, were growing more and more confusing and uncertain.

"Well I am," he murmured. "I'm very sorry."

Her spine straightened. She suppressed the sorrow she felt at knowing he considered her to be a mistake, telling herself it was ridiculous to feel that way. "I see," she said a bit stiffly.

"No." Geirwolf's gaze bore into hers. "You don't." He clasped her hands in his. "My English is not always so good. What I mean is, I'm sorry that I didn't realize how difficult of a transition this would be for you." He smiled. "My people have been capturing brides for a thousand years. And so I thought, in all my arrogance, that my way was the better way."

He snorted at that, then released her hands. "For this I am sorry because had I really considered your feelings I probably would have forced the lust I felt for you at bay and made myself take a bride from the women here. But I didn't and that truth cannot be changed. I can't be sorry you are mine, Peggy Valkraad, so please don't ask me to be, but I am sorry that you are unhappy that it is so."

Peggy nodded, his words making her feel more content than they perhaps should have. "And now?"

One of Geirwolf's eyebrows shot up. "Now that you are here how can I possibly regret the fact that you are mine? I could never send you away, Peggy. Never."

She gave him a half-smile. "Despite all my screaming?"

His smile came slowly, the twinkle in his eyes restored. "Yes, despite the screaming," he murmured.

They studied each other without speaking for a prolonged moment. Eventually Peggy glanced away, her sigh somewhat mournful. "Wolf..."

"Yes?"

"It does make me feel better to know that you're sorry I'm unhappy, but I just don't know that I can ever really be happy here. Because a part of me will always long to be free." She sighed again. "And resent you for not giving me that freedom back."

Geirwolf closed his eyes and took a deep breath. He opened them again and waited for her to make eye contact before responding. "I will not lie and say I would free you if I could because if faced with that choice I'm not certain I could be so selfless, but Peggy, you must understand that this choice is no longer mine. It never really was mine. Though I admit I planned to steal you all along."

She squinted her eyes at that. "I don't understand..."

"From the moment you clapped eyes on the men from the Hallfreor clan your choices had been taken from you." Geirwolf's eyes narrowed in a serious fashion. "The clans of New Norway have thrived for as long as they have for the simple reason that nobody knows of our existence. Whether I had desired you for my own bride or not, the warriors who accompanied me that day I stole you from the Hallfreors would never have let you go back from whence you'd come for fear you'd tell outsiders about our people."

Peggy chewed that over for a long moment, her thoughts and emotions in turmoil.

"I'm sorry you are unhappy, Peggy," Geirwolf murmured, "but there is no way my people will ever let you leave."

She took a deep breath and expelled it. For some reason or another, knowing that Geirwolf didn't have the power to let her go, that he'd never held that power, made it easier to let the anger toward him as a person go. She wasn't quite ready to let her anger with the people of New Norway in general go, but it wasn't the people of New Norway in general that she was married to. "So what you're saying is that we're stuck with each other and need to make the most of it?"

Geirwolf frowned. "You gave my words the grimmest possible connotation, but yes, I suppose this is what I am saying."

She chuckled softly at that, the twinkle back in her own eyes. "I didn't mean that quite like it came out but thank you for understanding."

Geirwolf took her hands in his again, his expression serious. "Please, Peggy," he murmured. "Let us begin again. Give me and our marriage a chance and I promise you I will never let you down."

Peggy bit her lip, her gaze locked with his.

"You won't regret it," he said softly, his lips coming down to kiss her forehead. "I vow it."

She closed her eyes for a threadbare moment, trying to sort out her emotions. When she opened them again she saw that Geirwolf was looking at her expectantly, waiting for her decision.

Her thoughts were in such chaos that Peggy ended up answering him without words. She couldn't seem to voice her feelings aloud so she told him what he needed to hear with her body.

Without giving it any more thought, Peggy gave into her instincts and let go. Turning around, she hoisted the furs up to her waist and, trembling from the cold, clutched onto a nearby wall while exposing her naked pussy to him. Arousal shot through her at the sound of her husband sucking in his breath.

"Peggy," Geirwolf said thickly. He came up behind her and roughly palmed her ass, kneading the two globes until they were warm and toasty. She could feel his eyes devouring her cunt, devouring her ass. "I'm glad you are mine."

She closed her eyes as he lowered his braies to his knees, her nipples hardening. The feel of the frigid air hitting her pussy coupled with the possessive way she could feel his gaze boring into her exposed cunt made her soaking wet and ready to take him in.

But Geirwolf didn't mount her. He stared at her pussy for a long time while his callused fingers kneaded her buttocks, as if memorizing the way her cunt looked. And then he sighed, a sound she wasn't certain what to make of.

Geirwolf let her buttocks go, then pulled the polar bear furs back down to cover her. "I'm a sentimental fool perhaps, but I can't take you like this. Not now." He patted her gently on the buttocks. "Not until I'm certain you truly want me."

Peggy closed her eyes briefly, stunned at the physical and emotional disappointment she felt at his words. Nevertheless, she made no protest when he took her by the hand and quietly walked her back to the breeding stalls. She supposed she should have felt embarrassed by the quasi-rejection, but oddly enough, she respected him more for it.

Life was getting very confusing, she thought on a shiver. Very confusing indeed.

Chapter 13

Two evenings later, Peggy came in from a day of watching other women be trained and opened the door to her private chamber. She found Geirwolf asleep on the bed, his big body sprawled out across it as he lounged on his back. Apparently he had come to her early tonight and had fallen asleep while waiting on her return.

She bit her lip. He looked so damn sexy just now, maybe even sexier than he looked when awake.

Her eyes flicked down to his groin. He was erect. Even in his sleep he still wanted her.

Peggy closed her eyes briefly, her emotions at war within her mind and heart. The tough-as-nails side of her, that side of her that had gotten her through her father's death and then again through college and graduate school, wanted to keep Geirwolf at bay forever just to prove that...well, she wasn't precisely certain what she was trying to prove. That she was strong perhaps? She sighed. Geirwolf had already told her at least ten times how much he admired her strength of spirit. So who was she trying to prove herself too? Herself perhaps, she admitted.

But the other side of Peggy, the nurturing side that wanted to love and to be loved, yearned to reach out to this man, to her captor...to her husband.

He was always so strong, she thought with admiration, her gaze flicking over the chiseled lines of his face. So strong and so kind...

Naked, her feet freshly painted and her pubic hair freshly trimmed, Peggy lowered her body to the bed and pulled

Geirwolf's braies down to his knees. His erection instantly sprang free, the thick piece of flesh pulsing as she palmed it.

"Peggy?" Geirwolf said softly, his tone confused. He blinked, trying to wake up. "What are you—" He sucked in his breath when she wrapped her lips around the head of his cock, whatever he'd been about to say long forgotten. "Peggy," he murmured, the fingers of one callused hand sifting through her hair. "That feels wonderful, my love."

His love.

Peggy closed her eyes and gave herself up to her feelings, to her desires. She took his cock all the way in, deep-throating it until it touched her tonsils.

"Ja," he breathed out, his muscles clenching as he twined tendrils of her coppery hair around his hand. *"Yes."*

She sucked him feverishly, her mouth and lips working up and down the length of his steel-hard cock in fast, suctioning strokes. The sound of saliva meeting flesh competed with the sound of her husband's breath catching.

"Ja," he gritted out, his voice sounding half-delirious as he possessively tightened his hold on her hair. "Sug kuken min," he said hoarsely, too far gone to speak in English. *Suck my cock.*

Peggy sucked him like a hungry animal, her face working furiously up and down the head and shaft. She brought her fingers into play as she sucked him off, massaging the sacs that lay tightly against his groin.

His moans grew louder as she took him in faster—deeper—harder—faster—deeper—harder...

"Peggy," he groaned, his muscles tensing and his eyes closing. *"My Peggy..."*

Geirwolf came on a loud groan, his jaw clenching and his teeth gritting. He spurted hot cum into her mouth as his entire body shuddered and convulsed, moaning as she drank it all up.

Peggy made a suctioning movement with her lips one final time, depleting the head of any remaining droplets. She swallowed it, then glanced up at him, her expression vulnerable.

Would he act smugly because she'd caved in this much? Would he behave arrogantly, knowing as he did the power he wielded over her?

"Thank you," he murmured, his voice humble. His wolf-blue eyes looked anything but smug and arrogant. They looked grateful. And at peace. "That was a precious gift you gave to me."

Peggy blinked, tears welling up in her eyes. "I—I'm scared," she breathed out. "I'm so very scared."

Geirwolf's eyes softened. "I know, baby." He held out his hands and pulled her down so she was laying on top of his chest. He kissed the top of her head, his hands gently stroking her back. "I know."

Chapter 14

One week later

Geirwolf's thoughts were in turmoil as he walked toward the breeding stalls. He hadn't touched Peggy in a sexual way for nigh unto a week for he wanted her to come to him when she was ready. Or at least for now, he mentally qualified, until her fears had been allayed.

But every night grew worse. Every night it became more and more difficult to resist the temptation of burying his rigid cock into her warm, pliant pussy or her talented, hot mouth…especially now that he knew what both of them felt like. He had no idea how or if he'd make it through even one more evening alone with her. He also knew, however, that he didn't want to frighten her, so he'd have to find a way to make it through the evening whether she wanted to be sexual with him or not.

Geirwolf didn't want to be an arrogant autocrat who took what he wanted when he wanted it, consequences be damned. His father had been that way when first his mother had been stolen, and if his grandmother's gossip could be replied upon (which it usually could) it had taken the jarl's wife a full four years to accept her place at his side. Four years was a hell of a long time—a lot longer than Geirwolf wanted to spend with Peggy feeling ambivalent towards him.

And so Geirwolf had held himself back, not wanting to make the same mistakes his father had made with his mother. The older couple was happy now, aye, but that happiness had come at the price of four years they could never get back.

The last week with Peggy had been wonderful in all ways except sexually. They were becoming friends, which was something he had never before experienced with a woman. He even felt comfortable sharing his feelings with her, which was something he had never before experienced with a woman or a man.

Geirwolf had been raised to be stoic and aloof, yet in a week's time Peggy had managed to penetrate all of the walls he'd spent a lifetime erecting. He had been raised to be autocratic and domineering, yet the mere sight of his wife made him feel tender emotions he wasn't entirely comfortable feeling.

He wanted her—more than he'd ever wanted anyone or anything in his life.

He was ready to be mated, and at thirty-four years was far past the age that most warriors reached before they took a bride. All of these years he had held himself back, hunting time and time again for a female who gave him the right feeling. Peggy was that female—he was sure of it.

He had watched her from afar for weeks, studying the way she interacted with others, studying everything there was to know about her. He admired her keen intellect, admired her independent, adventurous spirit, admired too the beauty of her lush, fleshy form. He had known the moment he'd clapped eyes on her back in outlander Barrow that she was the one. The weeks he'd spent studying her had only confirmed it.

The image of Peggy, naked and wanting him of her own volition, popped into Geirwolf's mind—again. He sighed, knowing it was but setting himself up for a fall to fantasize about an intimacy she wasn't yet ready to feel, but he couldn't seem to help himself.

He was already in love with her. He was beginning to wonder if she'd ever fall in love with him.

Geirwolf walked stoically toward the breeding stalls, realizing as he did that in the end the answer to that question didn't matter. They were wed. They would always be wed.

Peggy would always belong to him even if his love was never returned.

His jaw tightened as he considered the fact that it was possible his wife would never want him. He prayed to the gods that such would not be the case, but knew he had to prepare himself for that outcome.

Geirwolf prepared to open the door to Peggy's private stall, expecting to find her already asleep for he was coming to her later than usual. His hand stilled on the latch when the sound of soft moans coming from the other side of the door reached his ears. Stunned, he stood there in shock for a threadbare moment before a hot, all-consuming possessiveness coursed through him.

She has taken a lover. My wife is cheating on me...

Furious, and ready to kill whomever it was that was fucking her, Geirwolf pushed the heavy door open with all of his strength, inducing it to crash against the earthen wall. His heartbeat thumping like mad, adrenaline rushing through his blood, he stepped inside the dimly lit room, the sound of the door crashing shut behind him filling the small chamber. "What!" he bellowed, "is going on in—"

His body stilled as his eyes adjusted to the dim light of the chamber's single lit torch. He swallowed over the quickly forming lump in his throat as he watched Peggy masturbate on her back, her fingers gliding over her erect, slippery clit as she rocked back and forth in a slow undulation.

"I want you," she whispered. Her eyes were closed. Her voice sounded tired, a bit weary. "I'm sick of fighting it," she said hoarsely.

Geirwolf's mind now realized that no other male had fucked his wife, yet his body, still pumping full of primal adrenaline, hadn't quite caught up. His breathing was labored, possessiveness swamping him. She was laid out on the mating bed, her legs splayed wide apart, his for the taking.

Reacting instinctively, he came to her in a territorial fashion, pushing his braies down to his knees as he stood before her at the foot of the bed. Grabbing her thighs and pushing them apart, he entered her wet flesh without ceremony, seating himself to the hilt in one violent thrust.

"Fitta mi," he hissed, his teeth gritting. "My cunt."

Peggy gasped when Geirwolf thrust inside of her, then gasped again when he palmed her breasts and began to ride her body hard. Her husband had a menacing appearance every day, but tonight he looked downright dangerous, she thought. The tattoo of the dragon that snaked up his left arm seemed to move as his muscles flexed in time with his thrusts.

"Faster," she prodded him on. She had been given a week to sort out her feelings and now she wanted him so badly that even her nostrils were flaring. *"Fuck me harder."*

Standing before her at the foot of the bed, her legs spread wide apart by his callused hands, Geirwolf gave her what she wanted as hard as she wanted it. His fingers dug into the flesh of her thighs and his jaw clenched hotly as he buried his stiff cock inside of her pussy, over and over, again and again.

"Oh god," Peggy moaned, her head falling back and her back arching. She could hear the sound of their flesh meeting, the sound of her pussy sucking him back in with every upstroke. *"Oh god."*

"Come for me," Geirwolf ground out. He rotated his hips and slammed into her pussy harder. His fingers dug more securely into her thighs as he picked up the pace and fucked her with fast, merciless movements. *"Now."*

Peggy glanced down between her legs, watching as her husband's cock slammed into her flesh over and over again. The sight of his heavily muscled body holding her comparatively smaller one pinioned before him while his hips pistoned back and forth as he pummeled into her was the most erotic thing she'd ever laid eyes on. She came on a loud groan, her back arching and her eyes closing. *"Oh god."* Her head fell back onto the pillows, her nipples stiffening to the point of pain, her body convulsing. *"Oh my god."*

Geirwolf fucked her even harder then, the vein at his jugular bulging. *"My cunt,"* he ground out again and again as if it was a mantra. *"Mine."*

He went primal on her then, pumping in and out of her in fast, violent thrusts. He fucked her as if he was branding her, like an animal marking his territory.

Geirwolf impaled her pussy over and over, again and again. Perspiration dotted his forehead and his muscles clenched tightly as his body prepared for orgasm. The look of pleasure on his face—that expression that so closely resembled pain—held Peggy spellbound once again as he buried himself inside of her to the hilt in a series of lightning-quick, deep strokes.

"You're mine, Peggy," he growled, his teeth gritting. *"All mine."*

He broke on a loud groan, his body convulsing as he violently climaxed into her cunt. She threw her hips at him the entire time, using the movement to suck all of the cum out of his cock with her pussy. She kept the fast, furious movement up for a solid thirty seconds, not relenting until he collapsed on top of her with a moan, spent and satisfied.

It was a long while before either of them spoke. They simply laid there, holding onto each other as if the world had gone mad and they were each other's lifeboat to sanity. But then again, perhaps they were.

"I love you, Peggy," Geirwolf confessed. He placed a gentle kiss on first one of her stiff nipples and then on her lips. "I've waited my entire life to find you," he murmured. "And I hope that one day soon you will come to love me."

Peggy ran her fingers through his silky, sunny-blonde hair. "That's assuming I already don't," she whispered. She sighed. "And you should never assume anything."

Chapter 15

2 months later

It had been a long two months. Life in the breeding stalls was, after all, rather boring and monotonous. There wasn't much to do once your training was complete—other than watch other terrified women get trained during the days, then wait for your husband to come to you at night. And oh, how she had come to look forward to the nights…

Geirwolf was, for lack of a better expression, the best fuck on earth. He was attentive and possessed great stamina and had also, she thought with a small smile, turned out to be orally fixated—a fact Peggy would never complain about.

But it was more than the sex. It was also the talking. They talked a lot, she and Geirwolf. About everything and nothing. About the inane and the important. But mostly they discussed what their life would be like when she became pregnant and left the breeding stalls.

She walked toward her private chamber, knowing that Geirwolf would be coming to her soon, her thoughts on the conversation they'd had last night.

"I can't deny that I'm falling hard for you, Wolf," Peggy said, her hand absently stroking his chest. "But I also can't deny the fact that my work with the Inupiat is important to me. Or the fact that if I do become pregnant I would want my mother to be able to see her only grandchild."

"Peggy," he sighed. "I wish there was a way to grant you your desires. Yet my people would literally kill me did I try to take you from New Norway, if even for just a week or two."

"But Wolf…"

He held a finger up to her mouth. "The way our people have survived all these years is by remaining unknown to the outside world. No one who comes here – no one – is allowed to leave once they set eyes on New Norway unless it is to join the gods." He sighed. "I cannot say I am sorry you are mine, but what can I do?"

Peggy closed her eyes, her heart sinking. "Nothing, I guess," she whispered.

Geirwolf placed her hand on his erect cock. He wanted to be sexual again, any fool could figure that out, yet contrarily his thoughts seemed far away. His next words confirmed it. "The priests who serve as interim to the gods have declared for a thousand years that we are to live below-ground," he murmured.

Peggy's head came up. "Why?" she asked, genuinely interested.

"Visions they've had. Visions of a future earth where women are scarce."

Her eyes narrowed. "That's fascinating," she said truthfully. She was forever the anthropologist, always interested in myths and legends. "So they believe that by staying below the ground – "

" – That our people will never suffer this famine of females," Geirwolf broke in. "For we will continue to breed women in the numbers the gods intended, rather than become like the depraved who live above ground."

Peggy chewed that over, intrigued by the prophesies that had fueled the invention of this culture a thousand years ago. "Interesting," she murmured.

And, once again, Peggy had dropped the subject of her career and her mother. But even when she had caved in she had also realized that, inevitably, the subject would come up again. Like tonight.

Peggy sighed as she plopped down onto the bed. She had a lot of feelings swimming through her brain, all of them stemming from the knowledge that she was pregnant.

Pregnant, she thought, her heart racing. She was well and truly *pregnant*. Ivara had given her the exciting news this morning after she'd taken some primitive looking, yet highly accurate, test. By now even Geirwolf must know, she mused. So how did she feel about it?

Peggy raked her fingers through her hair, asking herself that question for the millionth time since she'd been given the news that she was to leave the breeding stalls tomorrow and go with Geirwolf to his home. On one hand she was elated, not only because she got to leave the boring stalls, but also because she was thrilled with the idea of having a baby.

And not just any man's baby, Peggy…Geirwolf's baby.

Geirwolf. She loved him—she was in love with him. He had gotten under her skin just as she'd known he would and had stolen her heart along with her body. And, just as Geirwolf had once predicted, she now held her hands out to him in the nights, wanting him to hold her, to love her.

Peggy bit into her lower lip, her thoughts a mess. On one hand she was elated to be pregnant, but on the other hand she was terrified. Being pregnant, after all, made her life in New Norway seem more…real. More real and more permanent. She was a true New Norwayer now, a full mate to the man who would one day rule the people here. She didn't know how to feel about that.

Being pregnant also meant something else, something that made her eyes tear up just thinking about the reality of it…

Being pregnant meant going through the delivery, and then through the joys and sorrows of motherhood, without sharing the experiences with her own mom. She knew Geirwolf disliked talking about these things for he felt as though his hands were tied where her mother was concerned, yet Peggy knew that a great sadness would always live inside of her without her mother in her life.

Growing up, her family had possessed little money but a lot of love. Her mom had worked two jobs after her father had died just to keep food on the table and a house over their heads. She had also worked her butt off to put Peggy through college. The fact that she was so close to becoming a Ph.D. was a point of pride her mother prattled on about to anyone who'd listen — and even those who didn't listen.

Peggy smiled, nostalgia overwhelming her whenever she remembered her mom. How could she be totally at peace, she thought, when her mother would never lay eyes on her grandchild?

"Hello little mommy."

Peggy glanced up from where she was sitting on the bed to a smiling Geirwolf. Her eyes lit up when she saw him, just as they always did. He was holding a gift wrapped in a silk covering, which she could only assume was meant for her. She supposed the gift was probably the gold arm bangles women were given to wear when they left the breeding stalls. "Hi."

Geirwolf's eyes narrowed. His gaze raked over her nude body then back up to her face. "You are...different today." His expression was stoic as usual, yet uncertainty lurked in his wolf-blue eyes. "Not so happy as I was hoping you'd be," he murmured.

"No — no! I'm very happy!" she quickly assured him. She shrugged, looking away. "Just not completely happy if you know what I mean."

"Your mother?"

She nodded. "Yeah."

He sighed as he sat down next to her on the bed. He was quiet for a moment, but then he said, "I want you to be completely happy about this baby — our baby. We made this child together and he or she deserves our devotion."

"Oh Wolf I know that." Peggy shook her head. "How could you think that I — "

He placed a callused finger to her lips. "I don't think that." He smiled. "But I want you to be happy." He sighed like a martyr, mumbling something about the unholy depths a man would sink to for his woman. "Your mother — she is widowed?"

"Yeah." Peggy's forehead wrinkled. "Why?"

"I just needed to be certain," he muttered.

Peggy gasped. "You're going to steal her?"

"Yes," he said without apology. "Since this is the only way you will be happy."

She didn't know whether to laugh or cry. "Steal her?" she whispered to herself, her feelings in overdrive.

The thought of her mother coming to live here—and being forced to walk around naked for crying out loud!—competed in her mind with the thought of her mother cleaning rich people's houses every day all day long just to make ends meet. And, worse yet, she believed that her only child was dead...

"Do it," Peggy murmured, hoping she was making the right decision. Her mother was a beautiful woman. The warriors here would be tripping over themselves to get to her. "Just promise me she won't end up in the Commons or the Dungeon of Shame." Her nostrils flared. "I mean it."

Geirwolf blinked. "Why should she dislike the Commons? And what in the world is a Dungeon of Shame?"

Peggy huffed. "Don't pretend ignorance. Ivara took us to both places and I know what they are."

Geirwolf smiled slowly. It was beginning to occur to him how it was that Ivara was able to break the reticence of brides down in mere hours. She lied to them. "Do enlighten me."

Peggy told him about her experience in the Commons and about how the men there touched any woman they wanted to. She told him about the blue-eyed devil who had pulled her down onto his lap and scared the wits out of her. (Geirwolf would be having a long talk with his blue-eyed devil of a brother.) And then she told him about the women who had been hung in cages in the Dungeon of Shame, splayed out on all fours for the use of any man who wanted them. By the time she was done talking, much to her disgruntlement, Geirwolf was laughing so hard he had tears in his eyes.

"How can you laugh about that?" Peggy squeaked. "It's deplorable!" This was the first time she'd ever seen him laugh and she had to admit he did it quite sexily.

Geirwolf grinned as he sat her nude body down on his lap. "That was all lies Ivara concocted. Truly, the Dungeon of Shame doesn't even exist." He chuckled again. "She must get some of her widow friends together for these little performances to scare the brides into relenting." One eyebrow shot up. "Pretty ingenious do you ask me."

Peggy frowned. "I can't believe I was taken in by that."

"I'm glad you were," he teased. "I was dying to breed you."

She shook her head, but couldn't help but to grin at that. "And the Commons?"

Geirwolf's expression turned serious. "It's a real place, but nothing non-consensual goes on there." He shrugged. "Only widows not bound to any warrior are permitted to go there. It's a place where they can do anything they'd like, sow their wild oats so to speak, before settling on another warrior."

"That's why their pubic hair is shaved? That means they are widows?"

"Ja—Yes."

Peggy chewed that over for a moment. She supposed it all made sense. The females she'd been trained with who had been native New Norwayers wouldn't have known about what went on in such a place because they were too young to, so that explained their fright as much as the fright of the non-natives.

She rolled her eyes and sighed. "Ivara's one smart cookie, I'll give her that."

Geirwolf chuckled at that. "It appears so." He shooed Peggy off of his lap and stood up. "Come. We can discuss this after we get you out of these damn breeding stalls. I've been waiting for you to be moved into our home for an age it feels like."

Peggy smiled, his dark, brooding accent sounding sexier than ever. "Me too." She couldn't wait to leave the stalls. She wanted to find out if Michelle had settled in well, she wanted to see her mother, and she admitted, she wanted to be with her husband on a full-time basis.

Geirwolf's body stilled. His eyes searched hers. "Are you really happy about the baby?" he murmured.

"Oh yeah." She grinned, then gently patted her tummy. "I can't wait to have your baby, Wolf. I hope she's a girl so she can give you major hell."

He smiled at that. "I wouldn't complain," he said softly. "I will love her. As I love you."

Peggy stood up on tiptoe and kissed the tip of his nose. "I'm glad you love me." She smiled. "Because I love you too."

Epilogue

5 years later...

Peggy Brannigan Valkraad had lived a charmed life thus far, a life that seemed to grow more and more charmed every day. Five years and two kids later, she and Geirwolf were more content than either of them had dreamed possible.

"Do you think you'll finally have a girl this time?" Michelle asked on a grin, her hand absently stroking her own round belly. Michelle was pregnant with her fourth child and Peggy with her third.

Peggy grinned back as they walked toward the bartering stalls together. "I certainly hope so. Of course, Wolf promised his brother Bjorn that if this one was a boy we'd name it after him since we named our first two sons after his father and next oldest brother."

"Aevar and Arne are little rascals. I'm not so sure you need to add another Valkraad male to their numbers," Michelle teased.

Peggy chuckled at that. "True enough. My mom and I are hoping for a girl this time."

"How is your mom anyway?" Michelle asked as they walked into a grocer's den.

"Great!" Peggy said happily. She thought back on when her mother had first arrived in New Norway a little over four years ago right before she'd given birth to Arne. Her mom had fallen almost immediately for Geirwolf's uncle, though she'd been hardpressed to admit it at the time. But then that was a different story. "She's pregnant, you know." Peggy grinned. "I'm going to be a sister again!"

Michelle gasped. "Nobody told me! That's great!"

"Yeah," Peggy chuckled. "Though mom still swears she's too old to be birthing babies like a savage. You know, without drugs."

The two friends laughed at that, then ventured further into the grocer's den. Peggy spotted Geirwolf almost immediately, their two boys sitting on either of his broad shoulders, pointing out foodstuffs they wanted.

Peggy smiled when her husband's wolf-blue eyes found her aqua ones. Already five years had gone by and she felt more attracted to him now than she did then. "You need some help, big guy?" she teased.

Geirwolf winked at her. "You best believe it. These two little warriors want everything they see. Pigs, the both of them."

She chuckled at that. She turned to Michelle and hugged her goodbye, promising to stop by her and Ragnar's cavern tonight for a game of cards after the boys went to bed.

Peggy's eyes flicked away from the grocer's den and toward the ice-coated stone door that lay a few feet away, hiding New Norway from the rest of the world. She smiled nostalgically, remembering the day not too long ago when she'd been brought to her home through that very portal.

"Are you coming, my love?" Geirwolf asked from behind her. "I'm wanting to barter for this bread. What do you think?"

Peggy turned on her painted feet, the ice-coated door forgotten. "I think I love you," she murmured. She smiled at his blush. "More and more every day."

"I love you too," Geirwolf said softly, his lips coming down to brush against hers. "And I'll show you how much tonight."

Peggy sighed contentedly, her smile dreamy as he threaded his fingers through hers. Geirwolf and Peggy Valkraad walked back into the grocer's den hand-in-hand, their two sons happily perched on their father's shoulders.

About the author:

Jaid Black is a novelist for Ellora's Cave, Berkley/Jove, and most recently, Simon & Schuster (Pocketbooks). Her earlier (steamy but not erotic) titles can be found under the pen name Tia Isabella. A single mother, Jaid and the kids enjoy traveling together as time allows. When Jaid gets her way, which usually involves a lot of begging and dire threats, they head toward Europe. When the kids get their way, which is usually the case, they head for Disney World.

In addition to writing erotic romances, Jaid also collaborates on horror novels and screenplays (horror and romantic comedies) with fellow EC author Claudia Rose. Their joint pen name is Millar Black.

Jaid welcomes mail from readers. You can write to her c/o Ellora's Cave Publishing at 1337 Commerce Drive, Suite 13, Stow OH 44224.

Also by Jaid Black:

Death Row: The Avenger

Death Row: The Fugitive

Death Row: The Hunter

Enchained

God of Fire

Manaconda

Politically Incorrect Tale: Stalked

Sins of the Father

The Hunted

The Obsession

The Possession

Trek Mi Q'an: Dementia

Trek Mi Q'an: Enslaved

Trek Mi Q'an: No Escape

Trek Mi Q'an: No Fear

Trek Mi Q'an: No Mercy

Trek Mi Q'an: Seized

Tremors

Vanished

Warload

Why an electronic book?

We live in the Information Age—an exciting time in the history of human civilization in which technology rules supreme and continues to progress in leaps and bounds every minute of every hour of every day. For a multitude of reasons, more and more avid literary fans are opting to purchase e-books instead of paperbacks. The question to those not yet initiated to the world of electronic reading is simply: *why?*

1. *Price.* An electronic title at Ellora's Cave Publishing runs anywhere from 40-75% less than the cover price of the <u>exact same title</u> in paperback format. Why? Cold mathematics. It is less expensive to publish an e-book than it is to publish a paperback, so the savings are passed along to the consumer.

2. *Space.* Running out of room to house your paperback books? That is one worry you will never have with electronic novels. For a low one-time cost, you can purchase a handheld computer designed specifically for e-reading purposes. Many e-readers are larger than the average handheld, giving you plenty of screen room. Better yet, hundreds of titles can be stored within your new library—a single microchip. (Please note that Ellora's Cave does not endorse any specific brands. You can check our website at www.ellorascave.com for customer

recommendations we make available to new consumers.)

3. *Mobility*. Because your new library now consists of only a microchip, your entire cache of books can be taken with you wherever you go.

4. *Personal preferences are accounted for*. Are the words you are currently reading too small? Too large? Too…**ANNOYING**? Paperback books cannot be modified according to personal preferences, but e-books can.

5. *Innovation*. The way you read a book is not the only advancement the Information Age has gifted the literary community with. There is also the factor of what you can read. Ellora's Cave Publishing will be introducing a new line of interactive titles that are available in e-book format only.

6. *Instant gratification.* Is it the middle of the night and all the bookstores are closed? Are you tired of waiting days—sometimes weeks—for online and offline bookstores to ship the novels you bought? Ellora's Cave Publishing sells instantaneous downloads 24 hours a day, 7 days a week, 365 days a year. Our e-book delivery system is 100% automated, meaning your order is filled as soon as you pay for it.

Those are a few of the top reasons why electronic novels are displacing paperbacks for many an avid reader. As always, Ellora's Cave Publishing welcomes your questions and comments. We invite you to email us at service@ellorascave.com or write to us directly at: 1337 Commerce Drive, Suite 13, Stow OH 44224.

Printed in the United States
29164LVS00008B/76-708